THE THINGS
FROM ANOTHER WORLD

THE THINGS
FROM ANOTHER WORLD

JOHN GREGORY BETANCOURT

A sequel to "Who Goes There?"
by John W. Campbell, Jr.

WILDSIDE PRESS

TALES OF THE THINGS

Who Goes There? by John W. Campbell, Jr.
Frozen Hell, by John W. Campbell, Jr.
Short Things, edited by John Gregory Betancourt

THE "THINGS" TRILOGY

The Things from Another World,
by John Gregory Betancourt

Mars is Hell, by John W. Campbell, Jr.
and John Gregory Betancourt
(forthcoming)

Earth Strikes Back,
by John Gregory Betancourt
(forthcoming)

Published by
Wildside Press LLC
wildsidepress.com

This book is dedicated to

EVELYN KRIETE

who went above and beyond to make this project happen;
and to

JOHN HAMMOND, KATEA HAMMOND,
and LESLYN RANDAZZO

who trusted me to bring a new vision to the Things;
and to my wonderful wife

KIM

who makes everything else happen.

AUTHOR'S NOTE

I am (as you should be, if you're reading this) a huge fan of John W. Campbell, Jr.'s classic novella, "Who Goes There?" and its many incarnations.

I first encountered the Thing at age 17, in high school, when my mother took me to see John Carpenter's classic *The Thing* the opening week in the local movie theater. She knew I loved science fiction, and she patiently sat through the blood and gore and mayhem so I could see the movie. By the time the final credits rolled, I was forever hooked on monsters and John Carpenter films. Who wouldn't be?

Of course, I already knew who the author of the original story was: John W. Campbell, Jr. one of my heroes. (I was a weird kid. My heroes were mostly editors: John W. Campbell, editor of *Astounding Science Fiction* magazine, which was now renamed *Analog*; George Scithers, editor of my favorite magazine, *Isaac Asimov's Science Fiction Magazine*; Donald A. Wollheim, editor of DAW Books, my favorite book line; and H.L. Gold, former editor of *Galaxy* magazine, whose back numbers I obsessively collected since finding a long run of 1950s issues in an antiques barn in South Dakota a few years before.)

Over my now 40-plus-years career, I was fortunate enough to have met Don Wollheim (and had a few of my short stories appear in anthologies he published); correspond with Horace L. Gold; and sell my own fiction to, work as an assistant editor for, and ultimately co-edit the legendary pulp magazine *Weird Tales* with George Scithers. The only childhood hero I missed was Campbell, who passed away at age 61 in 1971. But in many ways, he was the most important to me.

Why? Because Campbell single-handedly ushered in the Golden Age of Science Fiction. Almost every novel and short story I loved growing up had Campbell's fingerprints somewhere on it. Fritz Leiber's Fafhrd and the Gray Mouser series? Check. Isaac Asimov's Foundation series? Check. Frank Herbert's *Dune*? Check. A.E. Van

Vogt's *Slan*? Check. Robert A. Heinlein? Poul Anderson? Arthur C. Clarke? Orson Scott Card? A thousand checks! He edited and published them all—and hundreds more—over his career.

At his height, he completely dominated the science fiction scene and set the standards for everything that followed. *Astounding*'s circulation reached heights that no SF magazine comes anywhere close to these days. It wasn't till the 1950s that he had serious challengers as best editor in the field, with the launch of new, well-funded magazines like *Galaxy* and *The Magazine of Fantasy & Science Fiction*.

One thing people often forget, though: before he became an editor, Campbell was an author—and one of the best the field had produced up to that point. "Who Goes There?" (which introduced the Thing) was originally published in the August, 1938 issue of *Astounding* (although Campbell became editor in 1937, the story had been purchased by his predecessor; it appeared under a pseudonym, "Don A. Stuart," to immediate fanfare and became an instant classic.) Since then, "Who Goes There" has been reprinted dozens of times, translated into a score of languages, adapted into at least four film versions, and spawned one of the science fiction field's iconic monsters. Very little published before or since comes close to having this one story's impact on science fiction and popular culture.

Cut to the present.

Today, I am privileged to help John W. Campbell's daughter and grandchildren manage the Campbell literary properties—and one of our plans is to build on his literary legacy with new projects. To that end, I have already published *Frozen Hell*, a long-lost, alternate version of "Who Goes There?" (with an extra 45 manuscript pages of previously-unseen story) and *Short Things*, a collection of short stories by leading science fiction authors, in which they played with Campbell's iconic monster in new and surprising ways.

This new novel—the first of a trilogy—kicks off what Campbell would have called a "thought experiment." In writing it, I asked myself this question: *What if John W. Campbell had heard about actual events that happened in Antarctica and crafted his original story around them?*

That makes the events in his classic story (or, rather, a version of them) real in *our* world, and it places them into *our* history. It also allows the Things some leeway to differ from Campbell's vision of them. (He was, after all, writing fiction. You know how these creative types are, always playing fast and loose with facts.)

So, readers, take note: in the universe of *The Things from Another World*, Campbell's story appeared in *Astounding* in 1938. John Carpenter filmed it as *The Thing* in 1982. But those were fiction.

This is reality, set the day after tomorrow, when the first manned mission has reached Mars. Despite that, the world is little changed from today. Life goes on, as it always has.

When another spaceship is found in Antarctica, it sets in motion events that—well, I'll let you find out for yourself!

I had a blast writing it. I hope you enjoy it, too.

—John Betancourt
Cabin John, Maryland
November 16, 2023

MAP OF THE BASE

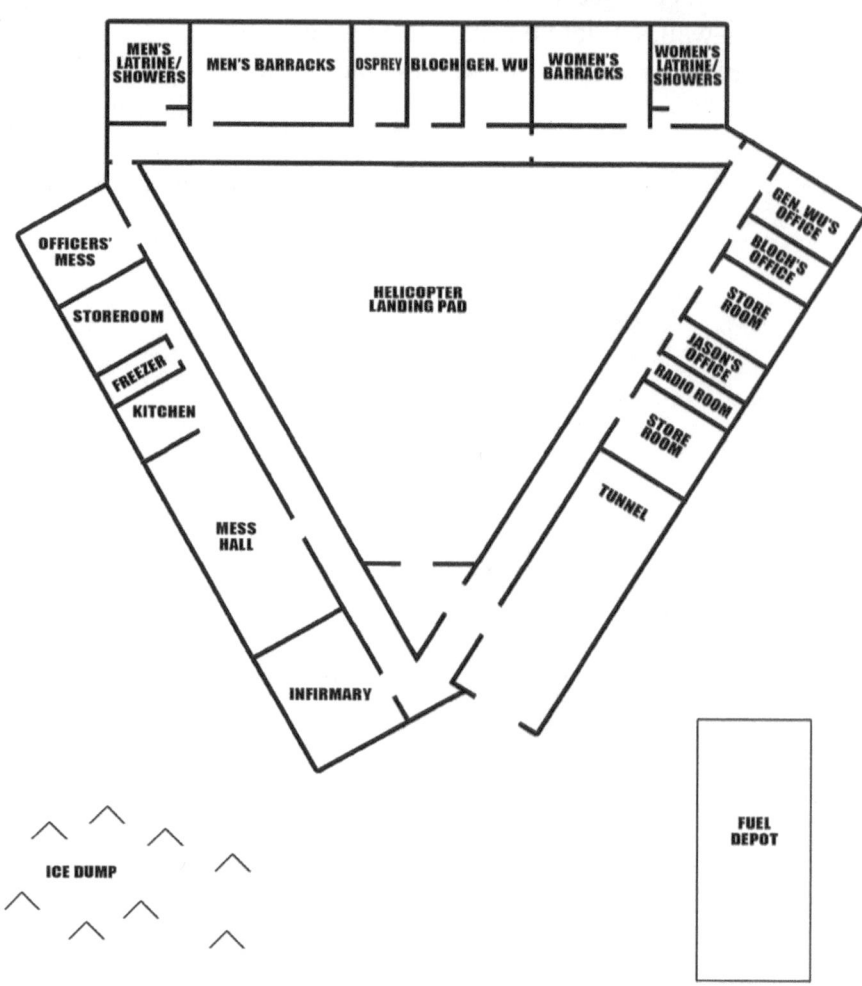

PROLOG

The Pentagon
Arlington, Virginia

General Artemus Wu bellowed for his secretary. Instead of Lieutenant Kirby, though, Colonel Bloch entered his office, shut the door, and quietly approached his desk. Bloch, with his beak of a nose and watery blue eyes that seemed to look through rather than at you, had never impressed the general as anything more than a pencil-pusher, the tiniest of cogs in the U.S. military machine. He was the sort of bland little career officer who rose slowly but steadily through the ranks, competent at every level but no more than that.

"Sir," Bloch said. His face remained stony.

"I assume from your presence here," said Wu, gazing at him over the black frames of his glasses, "that you are responsible for *this*?" With a blunt index finger, he thumped a stack of papers.

Typed on thin, age-yellowed paper, with a rusting staple in one corner, the report—dated October 29, 1938, and bearing the rubber-stamp marks of a dozen government agencies, plus a faded red CLASSIFIED across the top—clearly had been written by someone either crazy, on drugs, or both. A UFO buried in the ice in Antarctica…conveniently blown up, so no evidence remained? A telepathic monster that could absorb—and assume the shape of—any creature it encountered…also conveniently destroyed? Ridiculous.

"If you will allow me to explain—"

Wu sighed. "Explain what? How LSD made it to a military base in Antarctica? How some wise-ass wannabe sci-fi writer put his wet dreams down in a report for a lark? I'm less than a year from retirement, Ben. I don't have time for games." He threw the report at Bloch, who caught it. "Consider me pranked."

"They found a second one, sir."

Wu paused. "A second *what*?"

"Spaceship. In Antarctica. In the ice." Col. Bloch stepped forward and held out a manila folder. "The details are here. I wanted you to see the original report first to prepare you for this one."

Wu sighed again but accepted the new folder. Could it be real? Bloch had never struck him as the least bit imaginative. And his secretary, Kirby, wouldn't have had the balls to prank him.

Adjusting his glasses, Wu opened the folder, tilting his head back to study the satellite photograph on top through the bottom half of his bifocals. Antarctica, clearly. It had a geological map overlay, and an area two hundred miles east of the Amundsen-Scott South Pole Station had been circled in red. He flipped forward. More photographs. A dark shape deep in the ice, estimated—according to notations in the corner—at 148 feet long and 51 feet at its widest. Not a saucer. Sonar imaging showed a featureless oval. Thermal imaging showed nothing—the object was as cold as the surrounding glacier. Then came charts with technical calculations that he couldn't follow. A report on a core sample of the ice around the vessel finished up, dating it back almost 19 million years.

"If this is some kind of joke, Ben—" Wu began in a softer voice.

"No, sir. *Never*." Did Bloch actually sound offended?

Wu took off his glasses, rubbed his eyes. A year from retirement, and *this* had to fall into his lap. For now, he had to assume the report was true. And if it wasn't, God help Bloch, Kirby, and everyone else involved.

"How many people have seen this new report?" he asked.

"Six, sir. Three on my staff, two on the survey team. I am the sixth. You make seven."

Six others. Too many to keep this a secret long term.

"Has anything leaked out?"

"Not yet, sir. The survey team first reported it as a meteorite. Now they're not so sure. They are requesting confirmation from Caltech and NASA."

"A meteorite," Wu said. He put his glasses back on and leaned back in his chair, gaze distant. That sounded plausible. He nodded. Yes, that would be the cover story. "All right. We'll go with that. Get NASA to confirm it. Just a freak of nature, like the canals on Mars."

"Yes, sir."

The general held out his hand. "Give me that 1938 report again."

Bloch returned it to him, and Wu stuck it in the manila folder with the new report. He'd go through them both in detail again after lunch.

"Why haven't I seen this before?" he asked. It should have been in the officers' "funny file," which got passed around at meetings and parties. Letters from cranks, fake reports, FBI profiles of the president's cabinet…a UFO would have fit right in.

"It was misfiled, sir. Only came to light six months ago, during a records sweep under the Freedom of Information Act. It was a week short of being released…" His voice trailed off.

The general gave a bark of a laugh. Figured. Damned reporters were trying to release everything under the Freedom of Information Act. Good thing it hadn't gotten out. What a field day UFO crackpots would have had. For once, luck was on his side.

"How long does it take to get to Antarctica from here?" he mused.

"I'm not sure, sir. Three or four days, I would imagine. It's high summer in Antarctica, so conditions are optimal for travel."

"Find out." Wu leaned back. "Arrange whatever transportation we need. I want to see this thing for myself. You will join me, along with every member of your staff who knows about it. This must be contained. And lock down that survey team. Get them on our payroll. I don't want them communicating with anyone other than you and me…as a matter of national security. There should be enough money left in the discretionary expense fund to cover whatever it takes to buy their services. Civilian consultants. You know the drill."

"Yes, sir." Bloch hurried out.

Antarctica… Wu sighed. His wife would *not* be happy.
But if it's real…

CHAPTER 1

Army Corps of Engineers
Special Operations Base 1, Antarctica

"I *didn't* sign up for this," groaned Terry O'Reilly, throwing down his pickaxe and twisting first to the left, then to the right to stretch his back and shoulder muscles. "Months of digging, and all I've got are pains where I didn't know I had muscles."

"You and me both, brother," said Clay Washington. He had been—until three months ago—head of the Antarctic Geo-survey Team, as well as Terry's boss. They had both signed on with General Wu's team, helping to dig down through the glacier toward their discovery—whatever it turned out to be. A meteor? A spaceship? A frozen dinosaur whale (the wildest theory so far)? One guess was as good as another at this point.

He turned and gazed up the ice tunnel. Fifteen feet wide, ten feet high, with steel beams bracing the roof every six feet, it seemed to stretch to infinity, though he knew it only ran six-hundred feet to a switchback. The tunnel turned there, ran almost seven hundred feet more, then switchbacked again before finally reaching the surface, with its three semi-permanent buildings over the tunnel mouth.

Arc lights and space heaters set every thirty feet ran the entire length of the tunnel. Between the lights, the heaters, and the heavy digging equipment a hundred feet farther down, the tunnel temperature sometimes reached a toasty 30 degrees Fahrenheit, though mostly it lingered around 28. A series of wall-mounted fans hummed like a swarm of killer bees, circulating the air but doing little to relieve the months-old stench of human sweat and motor oil and exhaust fumes.

Terry sucked in a few more huge gulps of air. For a minute he paused to watch uniformed men with jackhammers attacking the wall of glacial ice at the end of the tunnel. Ice-dust and ice-chips flew. He and Clay had what the others called "the easy work," smoothing out the roughest parts of the walls so the mini bulldozer and the golf cart could pass each other in the tunnel with comfortable safety margins.

The glacial ice grew harder the deeper they penetrated. *We're measuring progress by the inch, not the mile,* he told himself. Even so, progress was steady.

A string of curses erupted behind him. He glanced over his shoulder at the team of Army engineers, struggling to reinforce a set of steel girders that had begun to buckle. No one wanted the tunnel to collapse before they reached their goal.

The clatter of the jackhammers abruptly ceased. Terry turned his attention back to the men who had been working on the wall. The mini bulldozer roared to life, zipped over, and began scooping up debris. It would ferry everything up to the surface and dump it a hundred yards from camp.

We must be getting close, Terry thought. He squinted at the rough wall of ice at the end of the tunnel. How much farther? The Army Corps of Engineers had mapped out a 7-degree downward ramp, and the team had turned the final corner two weeks ago. It should be smooth sailing the rest of the way.

Excited shouts rose from the men by the bulldozer. The driver cut its motor and climbed down from the cab. Everyone gathered in a circle, talking excitedly, but Terry couldn't make out the words.

Clay craned his neck. "I think they found something."

"Come on, let's take a look." Without waiting for a reply, Terry rose and ambled down to where men now gathered in front of the bulldozer's shovel. Finally something to break the monotony of digging and smoothing.

Clay jogged to catch up and fell in step beside him.

"—better call the general," Corporal Menendez was saying, as they joined the circle of workers. She was in charge of this work shift. "He's going to want to see this."

"He flew to the South Pole station this morning," someone said.

"Radio him. Hammond, take care of it."

"Yes, Corporal." PFC Hammond trotted over to a golf cart, got in, and zipped up the tunnel.

Terry stared down at a broken-off blade of metal jutting out from a chunk of ice as big as a man's torso. Under the bright lights, the blade gleamed silver. One side curved at a mathematically precise angle. Part of something round?

"That looks machined," he said.

"Yeah," Menendez said, glancing up at him. "Definitely machined."

Terry tried to visualize it whole. If the arc of its smooth side continued in a perfect circle, it might have been eight or nine feet across. Some kind of plate? Or…maybe a hatch? He swallowed hard.

"Give me a pick," Menendez said.

Terry found himself leaning forward as Menendez knelt, accepted a hand-pick from one of the men, and struck the block of ice as hard as she could—once, twice, a third time. Chips flew. Finally, with a sound like cracking knuckles, the block split in half, and each side shifted a few inches.

Menendez dug her gloved fingers into the gap and flipped the two halves apart, revealing more of the metal blade. The curved section extended another foot, then ended in jagged, twisted metal. Using the pointed end of the hand-pick, she pried it loose and lifted it free.

Standing, she turned the blade over, examining it carefully. Nobody said anything, but there seemed to be a collective holding of breath. Terry found himself leaning forward, straining to see.

"Well?" Clay demanded. "What do you think it is?"

"I've seen damage like this in war zones," she said slowly. "There must have been an explosion—a big one." She looked up, looked at the glacial wall behind her. "There's probably wreckage scattered all through the ice. But the weird thing…" She paused, swallowed hard. "The weird thing is, it feels like it doesn't weigh anything at all. Look!"

She dropped it—but instead of thudding to the ground, the metal settled slowly, like a feather drifting to earth. She picked it up and passed it to the next man, who repeated the experiment.

So it went around the circle. Terry got it last, after Clay. Just like Menendez had said, it felt like it weighed nothing at all in his hands. What the hell? He turned it over, tried to bend it, but couldn't. Strong and hard and cold. It didn't feel like aluminum, though. This was something else. Something new.

He returned it to Menendez, who hefted it, then used the blade of her pocketknife to try to nick off a piece. Other than a blood-chilling *scree-ee-ee*, her effort had no effect.

"Not even a scratch," she murmured.

Silence fell. Everyone stared—at the corporal, at the broken blade of metal, at each other.

Terry asked, heart skipping a beat, "*Is* it man-made?"

"Not...*man*," said Menendez slowly. "This is nothing I've ever seen before. Like nothing on our planet."

Terry barely contained a whoop of triumph. *Not a meteorite. Not a frozen giant whale.* It had to be a spaceship.

He turned and slapped Clay on the back. "It's *real*, man! We found aliens! We're gonna be famous!"

Then suddenly everyone was talking at once, babbling about aliens, spaceships, the strange piece of metal.

"Quiet down, quiet down!" Menendez suddenly bellowed. She had a voice like a drill sergeant when she needed it. Terry had only heard her use it once before to break up a quarrel in the rec room.

Silence fell like a switch had been thrown. The men straightened, turned to face her.

"We don't know anything at this point," she said. "I don't want to hear any crazy shit like aliens or UFOs. For now, it's just a piece of metal, nothing more. Maybe it's part of something, maybe it's nothing at all. Don't get ahead of yourselves. The general will know what to do."

"Are there more pieces?" Terry asked.

"Good question," Menendez said. She turned to look at the glacial wall from which the blade had come. "If we are entering a debris field, there should be more—a lot more." She gestured toward the ice. "Spread out and look. Use your lights. Sing out if you spot anything unusual."

The soldiers began unclipping flashlights from their belts. Terry remembered he had one, too, and fumbled it into his hands. The brilliant white LED beam was brighter than the overheads by a factor of ten.

Everyone moved forward and pressed the flashlight lenses against the ice, playing beams up and down through the glacier wall. Weird shadows shifted as light bounced from fracture mark to fracture mark.

"I've got something!" a man to his left called.

"Me too!" said another. "Looks like more metal. Maybe part of an I-beam."

"And here!" Clay shouted.

Six inches into his section of the wall, Terry's beam came to rest on something large and dark. He squinted. What was it? Not the silvery metal, certainly. A strange, black, vaguely fuzzy outline of… *something*. A walrus? The head of a mammoth?

He slid the beam up, around a shoulder-like curve, to what might have been a head…and then up and over to a single red eye, frozen open, that glared out at him from the depths of the ice.

CHAPTER 2

Amundsen-Scott South Pole Station
Antarctica

Welcome to hell, Jason Cosgrove thought.

A biting late-summer wind swept across the Antarctic Plain and hissed through the buildings of the Amundsen-Scott South Pole Station. According to the pilot of the airplane that had just dropped him off, local temperature was a balmy 12 degrees Fahrenheit. Jason already felt a chill penetrating his parka, two heavy sweatshirts, and thermal underwear, and tried not to shiver. Four layers weren't nearly enough.

Around him, the wind made a faint, whispery sound somewhere between fingernails on slate and snake-scales on glass, broken only by an occasional shout from the direction of the plane. Twelve different national flags, planted in front of the station's main building, snapped and cracked like whips. A few stray snowflakes swirled down from a leaden sky.

Jason dropped his two overstuffed satchels onto hard-packed snow, turned from the Basler BT-67 that had shuttled him here from Christchurch, via McMurdo Station, and stared out across what seemed an endless expanse of white. Only a lone black windsock and what looked like a couple of distant storage sheds broke the unending white of the landscape. An old joke popped into his head: *What's white and white and white? A polar bear eating vanilla ice cream in a snowstorm.*

He snorted and rubbed his eyes. Too long without sleep. Now he was getting punchy. He hadn't even gotten the usual layover in Christchurch.

A thousand miles of ice-desert stretched in every direction. Pictures online didn't prepare you for it. The huge, unending *bleakness* of it all. Even the sky seemed faded and dull by New York standards. The true ass-end of the Earth.

Shouldn't there have been someone waiting to meet him? He glanced back at the sleek mid-sized plane that had disgorged him minutes before. Its props still turned with a steady *whump-whump-whump*, as men and women in parkas bustled around the open door in its side. Supplies out, baggage in. And people. Lots of people. There had to be thirty-five or forty scientists and researchers queued up with luggage waiting to board. Going back to civilization before the six-month-long Antarctic night overtook the Amundsen-Scott Station and cut them off from the rest of the world. He alone had gotten out.

He turned toward the low sun and squinted. It was white as the snow and dazzling without the haze of pollution to filter it. Only a few more days till it began to dip below the horizon, dropping the temperature and plunging the Antarctic bases into hellish cold till spring.

"Doctor Cosgrove?" a man's voice called from his right.

Jason turned, eyebrows rising. "Here!" he called.

A tall, stocky man with a scraggly black beard jogged toward him. Unruly curls stuck out from under a green stocking cap, and he wore a puffy red coat zipped to the neck. The man thrust out a gloved hand, which Jason took. The fellow had a crushing grip.

"I am Milos Pappas." He pronounced it *MEE-los PAH-pahs*. His breath puffed visibly in the air. "I am the chief greeter for the station, and also cook. Very pleased to meet you, Doctor," he said.

"Call me Jase," Jason said. Everyone did.

"Jase, yes, good. I trust your journey was okay?"

Jason tried to laugh, but the sound came out like a crazy bark. He bit it off.

"No," he said, "everything was horrible. I hate to fly, and I'm here under protest. I've had maybe two hours of sleep in the last three days. I've been bullied into this, and—"

Milos raised his hands. "Not me! I am—how you say—only messager?"

"Messenger. Sorry." Jason took a deep breath and looked away. *Hold it together. Just a few more minutes...* "I don't like having to run to Antarctica to fight for my grant money."

"Fight?"

"I was told the funding for my research project might be pulled if I didn't get here within 36 hours to argue my case. Twenty million dollars for Asteroid Belt mining, gone—like that!" He waved one hand. "And no explanation why."

Milos shook his head. "Yes, the newcomers, they are—what is the word? Intense?"

"Newcomers?"

The man nodded. "They do not wear uniforms, but we know they are American military, all very top-secret hush-hush. They are here for maybe two, three months. Why the secrecy? I do not know, but all make guesses. One guess, it says they are excited for a meteor in the ice. Another guess, it says they are finding vast new oil fields. Me? I cook the food. Too many questions get you only trouble."

"Or saves your life," Jase said.

Milos considered, then grinned and shrugged. His gaze dropped to the bags at Jason's feet. "This is all you are bringing?"

"I didn't have much time to pack."

"I shall help you get the right stuff later. Plenty of everything in stores, with the main season at the end. But first, the big-dog newcomers wait for you." He grabbed both bags, turned, and lumbered for the main building. "This way, my new friend!"

* * * *

Jason found himself hustled through a series of hallways. It might be the end of their research season, but the base hummed with activity. He passed rooms full of people and equipment of every variety imaginable, a dining room with tables, and an empty rec room with a ping pong table, a pool table, and a jukebox. At last they reached a small conference room. There, two men with laptops worked side by side. They broke off their discussion—something about the Mars expedition?—as Milos swept in and dropped Jason's bags in a corner.

When the man on the right stood, Jason recognized him—Colonel Franklin Bloch. With his hawk nose, steel-gray hair, and coolly aloof gaze, Bloch made a lasting impression. He had been the one who Skyped Jason, informing him that his funding was under review and would likely be cut off if he didn't drop everything and get to Antarctica on the next plane. Or series of five planes, as it turned out.

The other man was of Asian descent and wore thick glasses with black plastic frames. His shaved head made guessing his age difficult, but he had the look of a man who had seen a lot of action over the years. He had also been on that video call, standing behind Bloch. He hadn't spoken a word, just studied Jase across the video link like a shark picking out its next meal.

"A pleasure to meet you in person, Dr. Cosgrove."Forcing a smile, Bloch came around the table and extended his hand.

Jase shook it, and found it disturbingly limp and moist, like shaking hands with a mushroom. After he released the hand, he had to make a conscious effort not to wipe his palm on his pants.

"I'm here. What's this about my funding?"

"Sit down, Jase," Milos said cheerfully. "I shall get you coffee?"

Jase glanced over, hesitated, then nodded. He could use caffeine. "Thanks. Black, please."

Milos glanced at the other two. "For you also?"

Both shook their heads. Milos headed for a Keurig machine on a table against the wall and began pushing buttons and fumbling with k-cups and a mug.

Bloch said, "This is General Wu. He's chairman of the Grants Committee."

"I thought everything was settled," Jason said, looking at Wu. "My project was approved with full funding six months ago. Why make me drop everything and rush out here?"

"Two reasons," Wu said. "First, I require the services of the best metallurgist available. Second, time is a factor. The weather is about to change, and I needed you here before it does."

Jason snorted. "If you want the best metallurgist available, you picked the wrong guy. You want Pieter Oud—"

"Dr. Oud died five days ago," Bloch cut in.

Jason stared at him. "That's not possible. He's barely forty—"

"Suicide," Wu said, studying his fingernails. "The Antarctic… did not agree with him."

"No way!" Jason's stomach seemed to plunge ten feet. He had known Pieter for the better part of two decades. They'd gone to M.I.T. together, taken a dozen classes together, partied together, worked off and on together over the years. Sure, Pieter liked to drink…liked it a little too much, sometimes. But suicide? It seemed impossible.

Gulping, he sank into the plastic chair. Pieter…dead. They'd talked only a few months ago, when they were at the New Tech conference in The Hague.

Then he realized what Wu had said. The *Antarctic* didn't agree with him.

"Pieter was here?" he asked, looking up.

"Yes. We need someone who can finish his work."

Bloch circled the table and slid back into his seat. Taking a sheet of paper from a manilla folder, he slid it across the table. He followed it with a silver Cross pen.

"Sign at the bottom," he said, "and we'll get moving."

"Black coffee," Milos said. He set a mug—WORLD'S BEST DAD! it proclaimed in big red letters—in front of Jason, then left, closing the door behind him.

Slowly Jason picked up the paper. A nondisclosure agreement. He'd signed a couple of them in the past, when he'd done corporate research, but this one struck him as exceptionally draconian. Matters of national security…prison and a multi-million-dollar fine if he so much as shared the project name… Crazy, all of it!

He shoved the paper away. "I can't sign this!"

"It is, of course, your choice," Bloch said, "but I strongly recommend it."

"Or you'll cut my funding."

General Wu shook his head, smiled. "I only said that to get you here." He spread his hands apologetically. "My daughter is on the Mars mission, and I'm a big believer in the space program. Mining the Asteroid Belt is a good idea. It's the next logical step, now that we have a toehold on Mars. I know we are going to need the raw materials there if our space program is to thrive. But you're still in the early planning stages, and your associates will manage everything just fine until you return. You can speak to them every day by secure sat-link, if you like. We have a far bigger project, one of immediate national importance, and we need your help *now*. Once you have the details, I have no doubt that you will agree that it must take precedence over everything else. Including asteroid mining. In fact, I guarantee it."

Jason snorted. "There must be a dozen other people available who would do as good a job."

Wu said, "No false modesty, Doctor. I need an American national, so that rules out quite a few candidates. And I need the best. Right now, that's you."

"Forget it," Jason said. He shoved his chair back and stood. "Now if you'll excuse me, I have a plane to catch."

"About that plane," Wu said, tilting his head. "Bad news, son. The one that brought you here is full for the outbound flight. We'll get you the next available seat, of course. Unfortunately, as you know, there are no commercial flights from this base, and passengers must leave as room allows. There is only one more flight scheduled this season, and I hear it's also fully booked. A spot for you might open up in the spring…by fall at the very latest. But look on the bright side. I understand you get a medal and a certificate from the station for wintering here."

"And possibly a tee-shirt," Bloch added.

"Or," said Wu, "you can join my team, be well compensated for your time, and do your country a service. A *vital* service."

Jason stared at him. "That's blackmail."

Wu smiled his shark smile. "No, Doctor. It's a job offer. A very good job offer, as you will discover. And as a good-will gesture, you have my word that I will continue to throw my full support behind your asteroid mining project when you return to the United States. You will find me a valuable ally."

Ally. Not a friend. Did Wu have friends?

"Can you tell me *anything* about Pieter's work?" Jason asked. "What was he doing?"

"It's classified." Bloch said.

I can't believe they're doing this, Jason thought. He ground his teeth and felt like punching something. Felt like he was teetering on the edge of a bottomless hole. *I can't believe they're going to strand me here, whether I want to work for them or not.*

Wu leaned forward and set something the size of a walnut on the table. It looked like a nugget of silvery metal. One side had bubbled and melted; clearly, it had been exposed to very high temperatures.

"What do you think of it?" Wu asked.

"Aluminum?"

"Not exactly."

What did that mean? Jason reached out and touched the lump of metal with his fingertips. Cool and hard, it had an almost greasy texture. He picked it up—and gasped. It was feather-light, even lighter than aluminum, or any other metal. He squeezed it hard, and it hurt his hand. He had half expected it to crumple.

"Where did you get this?" he demanded. His gaze flicked up. Wu's cool, steady eyes regarded him with what seemed amusement. "What is it, exactly?"

"You must sign the nondisclosure agreement first," Bloch said. He twitched the document forward again.

Jason took a deep breath. What would he be getting himself into? What had Pieter been working on? What was this metal, and where had it come from?

For a heartbeat, he stared down at the paper, then picked it up and read it a second time, slowly and carefully. The terms hadn't improved. But as the general said, it did specify compensation…twenty thousand per month, for the duration of his involvement with the project. It guaranteed six months of work, plus an option to extend employment for another six months by mutual agreement. It would mean wintering in Antarctica. But if Wu meant to keep him here, anyway…

Idly, he rubbed his thumb across the lump of strange, silvery, light-as-air metal. Metal like nothing he had ever seen or heard of before.

Pieter must have been working on it for the general. Were they mining it? Or did it come from that meteor Pappas had mentioned?

It was the discovery of a lifetime. The possible uses in aircraft— in spaceships—even for his own asteroid-mining project—stretched before him.

If it could be mass-produced, it would change the world.

He bit his lip. He *had* to be part of it.

He grabbed the pen and signed.

CHAPTER 3

En Route to Army Corps of Engineers
Special Operations Base 1, Antarctica

On the four-hour helicopter trip from the Amundsen-Scott South
Pole Station to the Army's base of operations, Jason barely noticed
Wu and Bloch's presence. The general sat up front, next to the pilot.
Bloch sat in the seat next to Jason, typing fast on a small laptop com-
puter.

"These are Dr. Oud's reports," the colonel had told him when
he settled into his seat behind the pilot. Bloch's voice sounded tinny
and distant through the headphones. He passed over a brown leather
satchel.

Jason barely nodded. He was already pawing through dozens of
composition books. Pieter had always favored working in composition books rather than computers since their college days. When he
found the book labeled #1, he flipped it open and instantly recognized his friend's tiny, cramped writing. The mix of block letters and
sloppy script was unmistakable. No one else kept notes like these.
He counted 16 books—more than a thousand pages of scribbled test
results, diagrams, theories, and guesses to go through. It would take
weeks to make sense of everything.

But as he skimmed one composition book after another, a pattern
began to fall into place. From what he could tell, Pieter had made
almost no progress. And after the first six books, clearly the Antarctic had gotten to him. His journal began to spend as much time
complaining about migraine headaches and night-terrors as it did
documenting tests on the metal fragments. It became less a working
research document than a personal diary. It painted a bleak picture of
a man slowly falling apart under immense stress and close confinement. Worse, no one at the base had recognized danger signs until
Pieter killed himself.

And the metal... It had defied analyses on so many levels, at least with the tools available at the army base. Pieter knew more about what it wasn't than what it was.

Harder than steel.

Non-radioactive.

Non-conductive.

Acids had no effect.

Pieter had guessed it contained exotic matter, but he hadn't been able to identify it with the equipment at hand.

The most interesting results came when he used a small foundry to discover its thermal properties. It melted at 637-degrees Celsius—roughly 150 degrees more than zinc, but 4.5 degrees less than aluminum. Given those properties, it shouldn't have been harder than steel.

Then, against all logic, it burned explosively at 893 degrees.

He dug out a pen and scribbled a few notes in the margins of Pieter's journal, then double-checked all the calculations. The energy output seemed to violate Hess's Law governing constant heat summation.

He sat back, eyes distant. That, or Pieter had made a series of gross mistakes and miscalculations. And that wasn't like Pieter. Or had his mental condition allowed him to get sloppy? He had been suicidal.

Jason turned the numbers and calculations over in his head, trying to wrap his mind around the implications. *Could* Hess's Law be wrong? Were there flaws in their basic, fundamental understanding of physics and thermodynamics?

He jumped when Col. Bloch spoke to him over the intercom:

"Dr. Oud got that same look the first time he tried to analyze the metal."

"There must be a mistake somewhere," Jason said, turning his head to meet Bloch's gaze. "His math is wrong. It has to be."

"Perhaps. Or perhaps we don't understand how the universe really works. Or, as Dr. Oud once said to me, maybe there are ways to get around the laws of physics."

"That doesn't sound like Pieter." He had always been a strict fundamentalist when it came to the laws of nature. Never a pie-in-the-sky dreamer.

Bloch cleared his throat, then proceeded to explain about the object found in glacial ice. "We suspect it came from a 19-million-year-old spaceship," he said flatly. "It changes everything we know about the universe. And it virtually guarantees the existence of faster-than-light travel."

"A...spaceship?" Jason gave a nervous laugh, only Bloch didn't seem to be joking.

"This is the second one we've found."

"No shit?"

"Scout's honor." Solemnly, he held up three fingers. "Researchers studying a magnetic anomaly found the first one in 1938. They accidentally blew it up when they tried to melt the ice with thermite."

Jase snorted. "That was a monumental bit of stupidity. Thermite burns at more than 4,000 degrees."

"It was a different age." Bloch shrugged. "They were trying to melt the ice to get to it. They weren't prepared the way we are."

"How come word never got out?"

"Hard to prove, when you've blown up the evidence." He laughed without humor. "A report *was* filed. It got classified and forgotten. But someone must have heard about the spaceship. There was a sci-fi story published that year by a writer named Campbell which follows the script pretty closely. Luckily everyone thought it was fiction."

Jase said, "Tell me about the metal."

"We have a team from the Army Corps of Engineers tunneling down to the spaceship now. They are cutting their way through a glacier, but it's slow going because the ice is so dirty."

"Dirty?"

"Full of rock and dirt thrown up by the impact from the crash. But they found a few small lumps of the super-light metal. More than enough to keep us digging for more."

Jason rifled through the journal pages. "Pieter destroyed...let's see...at least two of the fragments during testing, when they caught fire in his lab. How many others are there?"

"Fragments? A half dozen more."

General Wu broke in, his voice tinny over the earphones. "News from the team at the base. They seem to be entering a larger debris field." He turned in the front seat and faced Jason for the first time since they had left the Amundsen-Scott Station. "I just received word of several new discoveries over the radio."

Jason leaned forward. "More of the metal?" he asked.

"At least one much larger piece, yes."

"Great." They needed as many samples as they could get, especially with two of them destroyed. "You have to get it to a lab with a scanning electron microscope." He paged back through one of the composition books, looking for a passage he'd read half an hour before. "Pieter thought there might be something screwy with it on the molecular level. Some sort of forced bond that shouldn't occur—*can't* occur—in nature. He thought it might involve exotic matter—"

There was a sharp click on the audio channel, and the general faced forward again. Jason could see him talking, but couldn't hear anything over the roar of the copter's rotors.

Bloch had heard him, though, and shook his head. "Negative of the outside testing. We can't let anything out of our hands at this point. The general doesn't want word of the discovery to leak out prematurely or every major power in the world will descend on us, trying to get a piece for themselves. You have to do everything you can on site, at least for now."

"Pieter's notes complain over and over that facilities are inadequate."

"As I told Dr. Oud, make a list. I will do my best to get everything you need, if it's at all possible. It may take a while, since we have to go through Army procurement channels, and we are trying not to attract undue attention. But your work is of utmost priority for the general."

Sighing, Jason looked down at the papers in his lap. No sense arguing; Bloch and Wu clearly meant to keep this discovery under wraps for now. He'd survey the lab and make a list of anything that might prove helpful. Perhaps it wasn't as dismal as Pieter said. Could Bloch get him a scanning electron microscope on the DL? Perhaps. But he doubted it.

Never mind that what he really needed was a complete state-of-the-art research lab like they had at Cornell or CalTech. What could he do at an army base that Pieter hadn't already done?

Jason chewed his lip and gazed out the window at the icescape flowing endlessly below. The copter cast a long shadow to their left, and it rippled over small bumps and fissures, the only dark feature in this impossibly bleak land. Not an animal in sight. Not a landmark. Just white. The old joke came back to him, what's white on white on white? *A polar bear eating vanilla ice cream in the snow.* But here they didn't even have a polar bear.

Slowly the reality of what Bloch had told him sank in. *Could* the metal be from a spaceship? It seemed incredible. Impossible.

And yet…

He raised the lump of metal. And yet, as he touched that bubbled, half-melted bit of alien debris, no other explanation seemed to fit.

* * * *

An hour later, hills of heaped-up mounds of freshly excavated rock and snow came into view. The copter slowed.

"This is our base," Bloch said.

"Does it have a name?" Jason asked.

"Just a string of numbers."

Jason had only a few seconds' look at three long, squat buildings arranged to form a triangle before the helicopter descended toward a snow-encrusted landing pad located in the center between them. The sun, its red-gold edge already dipping below the horizon, vanished behind fifteen-foot-tall corrugated steel walls.

Bloch touched his arm and pointed toward what looked like a small airlock in one building. "Put on your ski mask and gloves," he said, voice crackling over the radio. " We don't have far to go, but it's well below zero here. We've already had a couple of frostbite cases. Bring Dr. Oud's papers, leave your gear. I'll have it brought to the barracks."

"Barracks?"

"That's what the troops call it. Dormitory. Communal sleeping hall. One name's as good as another.'"

Jason nodded and took off the heavy headphones. The roar of the copter rose to deafening levels. Quickly he pulled on a heavy black ski mask, goggles, insulated gloves, and the heavy thermal parka that Milos Pappas had given him at the Amundsen-Scott Station. The station had a good supply of clothing abandoned by former researchers who never intended to return. That, plus three unopened packages of thermal underwear, insulated leggings, and several used-but-clean sweatshirts, would supplement the cold-weather gear he had brought from home.

General Wu, well muffled in his own thermal clothing, had already climbed out and was striding briskly toward the building, his laptop tucked under one arm. Bloch stepped down, ducking well below the rotors circling overhead, and gave Jason a hand to the ground. Jase ducked, too, and followed him toward what looked like a small white airlock set in a corner where two of the buildings came together.

They entered a room about the size of an elevator and shut the door behind them. Here, Bloch pulled off his ski mask, and Jason slowly followed suit. His breath plumed in the air, but it was nowhere near as cold as it was outside. Next they passed through a second door, into a room lined with benches. Hot air gushed from wall vents. It felt like the blast of a heat furnace after the Antarctic chill.

Jason's eyes started to water, and he blinked and rubbed them. Parkas, ski masks, boots, and other cold weather gear had been hung on hooks or stowed on high shelves.

Then the stench hit. A sour mingling of human sweat, old food, body odor, and other smells Jason couldn't begin to identify. He half gagged.

"God!" he gasped, covering his nose with the ski mask. He took a step backwards. "What the hell is that stench—"

"In a day or two, you won't even notice," Bloch said flatly. "Living in close confinement, in a sealed environment, there's little you can do about the smell. It's far worse on submarines, trust me. At least we can vent in a little fresh air here."

Bloch finished hanging up his gear and waited while Jason did the same. Then he led the way into a corridor barely wide enough for two people to pass each other. Fluorescent light panels glowed overhead, revealing plain pale gray walls and bare plywood flooring. There were no windows, just a few doors. Clearly the army didn't feel the need for an interior decorator.

"Grim little place you have here," Jason observed. *No wonder Pieter killed himself.*

"It's built for practicality and survival," Bloch said. " Every exterior wall has a foot of insulation. Even with a catastrophic power failure, we could survive inside for days or even weeks, if necessary."

"But you're not expecting problems?"

"Of course not. The Army Corps of Engineers doesn't like to take chances, especially in extreme environments." He pointed to the right. "Mess hall, infirmary and rec room that way, in the next build-ing. He nodded to a set of double doors opposite them. "These lead to the tunnel. We've dug about six hundred feet down so far." Turning, he led the way to the left. "This building also houses your lab, offices for the general and me, the radio room, and several storerooms." He pointed ahead. "At the end of the hallway, turn left to enter the bar-racks building. Sleeping quarters and latrines are located there. No one has to go outside. Not that you'd want to, in this weather. And especially not when it turns bad. Keep going and you can enter the third building."

"Rec room, mess hall, and infirmary. Check. A big loop. Not complicated."

"Correct."

What have I gotten myself into? Jason thought. *I must have been crazy to sign up for this.*

"And here we are." Bloch stopped in front of a steel door. Some-one had written "LAB" on the wall beside it in thick black magic marker. Under it, someone else had written, "The Doctor Is In-Sane" with a much thinner marker.

"Someone's idea of a joke?" Jason asked. "I don't think it's fun-ny."

"Huh?" Bloch blinked at him.

He nodded at the sign. "'In-Sane'."

"I believe Dr. Oud did that. He worked himself pretty hard, and he was always in his lab coat, with his hair kind of, ah, crazy—if you'll pardon the expression. Some of the soldiers started calling him 'the mad scientist.' He embraced it."

"I can see him doing that." Jason nodded slowly, more to himself than to Bloch. *Just like Pieter to co-opt a joke at his own expense.*

Pushing the door open, Bloch reached inside and thumbed a switch on the wall. Overhead, fluorescent lights flickered and hummed to life.

"Welcome to your new home," he said.

Jason stepped past him and turned slowly to take in every detail about the tiny room. It couldn't have been more than eight feet wide, though it was at least twenty-five feet long. Crammed up against the walls sat a pair of narrow worktables covered with a jumble of equip-ment that looked like rejects from a salvage yard. A battered old laptop with a bouncing Windows 95 logo as its screensaver seemed to mock him.

"You've got to be kidding," he said.

CHAPTER 4

Army Corps of Engineers
Special Operations Base, Antarctica

General Wu pulled on black leather gloves as he entered the mouth of the ice tunnel. It sat inside the third of the three prefab Army buildings. His breath steamed in the air as he paused to look around. Small electric heaters kept the tunnel—and the building behind him—at a steady just-below-freezing temperature. This building existed solely to provide sheltered access for workers entering and leaving the work area below.

A cargo-container-sized airlock on the building's outer-facing wall also provided access to the ice-field a hundred yards from camp, where his fleet of mini bulldozers—could you call two a fleet?—dumped debris from the tunnel excavation.

Corporal Menendez had been waiting for him beside the golf cart. She straightened and saluted as he entered.

He returned the salute. "Status report?"

"Sir. We have recovered three more pieces of the metal. I had them moved to the holding area, per standing orders. Radiation test negative. Two more appear to be accessible and can be dug out with a few more hours' effort. One of the recovered pieces shows signs of machine-work. It may be part of a hatch or an airlock. And…" She hesitated.

He settled into the passenger seat of the golf cart. The vehicle rocked once, then steadied.

"Spit it out," Wu said. "What couldn't you tell me over the radio?"

"We found something else."

"Damn it, found *what*? I don't have time for nonsense, Corporal."

"Some…*thing*. A…a *creature*, I guess you'd say, frozen in the ice. It's…it's…" She shuddered, looked away. "You can't see it too clearly, but what you can see— I'm sorry, sir. It's like something out of a nightmare."

Wu felt a stab of panic as he remembered the report he'd read at the Pentagon. Remembered how the 1938 researchers found an alien creature frozen in ice and thawed it out, only to have it come to life. Nineteen million years frozen, and it came to life!

The possibilities boggled the mind. He had never dreamed they'd find one of the creatures here. He felt his jaw tighten. It had to be contained. And then it would have to be destroyed. Fire would be best—it would have to be incinerated to the last molecule. He could take no chances with it. If it still lived, if it got loose—no, he couldn't let that happen. It had to be destroyed as soon as possible.

Keeping his voice steady, he said, "You didn't dig this creature out yet, did you?" He found himself holding his breath.

"No, sir."

"Good." That was a relief. He had time to deal with it.

Nodding slightly, he gestured toward the tunnel. "Let's go. I want to see everything."

Menendez climbed in next to him, put the golf card in drive, and accelerated. As the little vehicle hummed down the incline, ice wet-glistening walls closed in on every side. The car's electric motor hummed faintly. Ahead, puddles of illumination from overhead arc lights forced back the darkness every fifteen yards.

"Is this creature blocking the tunnel path?" he asked.

"Partly, sir. But I think we can go around it, if necessary. And—if you don't mind—maybe I can cover it with a tarp?" Quickly, she added, "Most of the soldiers find it unnerving. And it really freaked out the civilians, especially O'Reilly."

Damn…he had forgotten Terry O'Reilly and Clay Washington had been assigned to work with the excavation crew. Would this discovery make them more of a liability? Men had been known to violate non-disclosure agreements when the payoff was big enough.

He said, "I'll take it under advisement." He looked into the distance, gaze unfocused. A tarp…probably a good idea. The fewer people who saw the creature, the better. And no one would be able to take cell phone pictures. Less to deny later. There could be no proof of its existence once it was incinerated. No photos—other than his official ones, of course.

When they turned at the first switchback, Wu realized he hadn't seen any workers yet. Nor could he see any in the stretch of tunnel ahead. Just more arc lights and orange-glowing electric heaters.

"Where is everyone?" he asked.

"At the discovery site, sir. They all wanted to see it."

He sighed, shook his head. Understandable, though. The team had been working for two months with no real discoveries beyond those few small lumps of strange, alien metal to break the monotony. Of course they'd all want to check out a frozen, alien monster. In their place, he would have done the same.

Corporal Menendez turned at the second switchback, then Wu spotted fifteen or so people at the far end of the tunnel. All work had ceased, but the gathering didn't have a festive atmosphere. If anything, the crowd struck him as overly hushed and subdued…almost funereal. Certainly not happy.

They spotted him coming and called to each other, snapping to attention. Menendez pulled the golf cart to a stop. Wu climbed out and returned the salutes. As he strode forward, the crowd parted silently, clearing a path to the rough-hewn wall of ice at the end of the tunnel. To the right, a section roughly a yard square had an inch-deep channel etched around it. For a second, it reminded him of a picture frame. And it framed…what? He squinted. All the arc lights had been angled away; he couldn't see much, beyond a dim, shadowy hulk perhaps three or four inches within.

Frowning, he swept his gaze over the whole team. No one met his gaze. Didn't they want to see their discovery? Even the two civilian geologists looked distinctly uneasy.

"Flashlight," he said, sticking out his hand.

Someone handed him a small Maglite flashlight. He thumbed it on, strode forward, and pressed the lens directly against the ice, angling the beam first up, then down, then across. Definitely something. Could that be…a head? He squinted, shifting the beam a few inches to the right. Possibly a head, but one covered with a mass of reddish-brown, thumb-like worms. Then the light caught a gleam of ruby red, and he turned it on what could only be an eye. It seemed to be staring straight back at him.

His stomach churned, and he almost dropped the flashlight. He took a step back, looked around at his soldiers. Now he understood. They felt it, too. An overpowering, visceral urge to destroy the thing in the ice. To smash it, burn it, grind it to dust. It was a primitive, from-the-gut reaction, an absolute *need* to see it dead and gone.

Skin crawling, he snapped off the flashlight, tossed it back to its owner, and forced himself to walk to the golf cart at a calm and unhurried pace. No doubt about it. This had to be the same kind of creature from the 1938 report.

And it had to be destroyed.

"I want it left strictly alone," he told Menendez, but he made sure his voice carried to every man and woman present. "We'll swing the tunnel to the right and go around. No one is to touch this wall or dig an inch closer to—to this sea lion—or *whatever* it is—for now. I want a guard posted day and night to make sure. It must remain in place until further notice. No one touches it. Understood?"

"General?" said the blond geologist, O'Reilly. "We were talking about cutting it out. That isn't a sea lion. With a find like this, shouldn't we—"

"No!" That sounded too sharp, too panicked. He cleared his throat, then added in a normal tone, "It may be carrying bacteria or viruses that could prove dangerous to modern life. I'll bring in a hazmat team to deal with it." *A hazmat team with a portable crematorium.* "No point in taking any chances. It's been here millions of years—a few more days or weeks won't matter all that much."

He glanced around at Menendez and her team. "I think we've all had enough for today. Let's knock off early and head back up to base. I'm declaring a holiday. I think we can break out a keg of beer from storage. Have some fun."

As expected, everyone cheered. But even the cheers seemed strangely subdued.

He hopped back into the golf cart.

Menendez called orders, assigned a three-hour guard shift to PFC Dobbs, told another man to cover the thing in the ice with a tarp, then climbed into the driver's seat beside him. Without another word, she put the cart in gear and floored the accelerator. Barely faster than a man could walk, they hummed up the tunnel toward the surface.

CHAPTER 5

PFC Hector Dobbs scuffed at the ice floor with the toe of his right boot as everyone else started the long trek up to home base. Just like that bitch Menendez to pick him for guard duty. Like that thing in the ice would be going anywhere…or anyone would want to dig it out. Now he'd miss most of the fun. Well, at least she'd only given him a three-hour shift.

He pulled a battered old .mp3 player from his breast pocket, shoved earbuds into his ears, and pressed the play button. It might not be as fancy as an iPod or an iPhone, but it played nearly two days of audio without recharging, and that's what counted down here.

As Metallica blasted his eardrums, he gave Menendez the finger—though she'd probably already reached the surface—played air guitar for a few seconds, then climbed onto the mini bulldozer's bucket seat and shifted until he found a comfortable position on the worn plastic. Better than standing or sitting on ice for hours.

So cold…

He shivered. It *was* cold.

His gaze drifted back to the tarp. Those two civvies doing make-work on the walls had wanted to dig it out. They'd gotten real hard-ons when that big chunk of metal turned up, whooping and hollering about aliens and UFOs. Yeah, right. Fucking *aliens*. The thing in the ice had to be some kind of sea lion, like the general had said, or maybe a walrus. Probably died of some disease. That would explain the red eye. He'd had pink-eye a couple times as a kid. Same thing, right?

He yawned. Although two layers of thermal underwear normally kept him pretty comfortable down here, it felt colder than usual now. He glanced up the tunnel, at the pools of light dotting the way toward the surface. Nothing moved.

So cold…

His gaze fell on the closest of the half dozen industrial heaters at the work area. Its heating element glowed faintly reddish-orange.

They needed a few dozen more of *those* babies.

As Kirk Hammett riffed through "The Day That Never Comes," Dobbs's mind started to drift. Metallica faded. The tunnel blurred. He closed his eyes.

So cold...

He barely noticed as he pulled out the earbuds and dropped them onto the seat, climbed down from his perch on the mini bulldozer, and crossed to the closest of the gently whirring heating units. Without thought or hesitation, eyes dull and unfocused, he grabbed the handles, tilted it back, and wheeled it toward the end of the tunnel. The heater's bright yellow power cord unspooled behind him with a faint whisper of sound.

So cold...

After dragging aside the tarp, he pointed the heater toward the thing in the ice, adjusted the setting to "High," and then returned the mini bulldozer. There, he settled back into his seat, closing his eyes and drifting into sleep. The soft, soothing sounds of dripping water and the faint *snap-crack-snap* of warming ice began to rise behind him.

CHAPTER 6

What have I gotten myself into? Jason Cosgrove wondered, as he plopped down on a narrow steel cot—one of eight along the left-hand wall of the room—and tried to breathe through his mouth instead of his nose to avoid the stench. If possible, the foul smells seemed worse here in the dormitory. More cots lined the right-hand wall. Too many sweaty, hormonal young men crammed together for too many weeks or months in too small of a space. Maybe they couldn't smell themselves anymore, but *he* certainly could. Each and every one of them.

The "male barracks," as Bloch had called this room, housed four-teen men—the soldiers, the cook, and two—no, three now—civil-ian contractors. *That's me—civilian contractor extraordinaire,* Jason thought. *Researcher into alien metals. Reluctant hero. Army dupe.*

At least the male barracks weren't as gray and sterile as the rest of the base. Here, soldiers had taped pictures of girlfriends and fam-ily members over their cots, or posters of women in sexy poses. One showed a barely-dressed woman at a piano, while another had a woman crawling on all fours trying to look seductive. A couple more showed tawny-haired women in bikinis, but he didn't recognize any of them. Pop stars? Models? Actors? He rubbed his eyes. He was get-ting old and out of touch.

The room was almost deserted. Two men in olive-green boxers and tees dozed on cots on the far side of the room, while another sat with his back to the wall and pecked with one finger at a bat-tered iPad. A fourth was thumbing through an old *Sports Illustrated* magazine. The man with the iPad had given Jason a quick "Yo!" and a wave of welcome when he came in but hadn't gotten up or intro-duced himself.

"Hey," he'd said back.

Stifling a yawn, he looked around the room. Battered olive-green trunks sat at the foot of each cot. Most of these trunks had names stenciled on them. His had masking tape with Pieter's name written on it in black Sharpie. No one had bothered to remove the tape before his arrival. His two bags sat on the cot.

If it hadn't been so sad, it would have been funny.

Pulling the tape off the trunk, Jason wadded it up, then didn't know what to do with it. No trash can in sight. He stuffed it into his pocket. There would probably be a trash can in the dining room.

Colonel Bloch, General Wu, and the base doctor slept in "Officer Country." Someone had scrawled those words on the wall in marker next to their private rooms. Rank had its privileges, after all. Beyond Officer Country lay the "female barracks" for the six women engineers.

"Hey," said a deep voice to his left. "We got fresh blood."

Jason leaped to his feet and turned to face the speaker—a tall, broad-chested African American dressed in coveralls and a black turtleneck. He had been speaking to a shorter man with red-blond hair and large, piercing blue eyes. They must have just entered.

"Hi," Jason said, sticking out his right hand. "I'm Jason Cosgrove. Jase."

"Clay Washington." He shook hands with Jase, then gave a jerk of his thumb. "This is Terry O'Reilly. We're civilian consultants. Geologists."

"Pleased to meet you." O'Reilly shook hands with him, too.

"Did you just get in from Amundsen-Scott?" Clay asked, then he laughed and shook his head. "Never mind, dumb question. Everyone comes through Amundsen-Scott. You don't look like you're army. Let me guess—metallurgist?"

Jason nodded. "I'm supposed to analyze some exotic metal you found."

The two men exchanged pointed glances. Then Terry plopped down on the bed across from Jason.

"Something wrong?" Jason said.

"You're Pieter's replacement, then."

"Uh, yes." His voice cracked a bit when he said, "Pieter and I went to school together. He was one of my best friends."

"Good guy," Clay said. "I liked him. A lot. We played cards almost every night."

Jason looked up. "Did he really commit suicide?"

"Hanged himself in the kitchen," Terry said. "Cookie found him when he came in for breakfast prep. The army guys had to cut him down. We never saw his body, thank God, but we heard all about it."

"He used a thin nylon cord," Clay added, voice growing husky. He looked away. "Nearly cut off his own fool head with it."

"Shit." Jason swallowed hard, looked away. What a horrible way to go. "But I never saw him as the suicide type. Maybe work himself to death, sure. But kill himself? Not in a million years."

Terry said, voice low, "It's this place. It messes with your head. Half the men in this room have night terrors. Hell, *I* woke up screaming twice last week. I'm just grateful I don't remember my dreams."

"I can see why," Jason said, glancing around the room. "This place is enough to drive anyone nuts. The stench alone—"

"Oh!" Clay said, brightening a little. "I can help with that."

He went to his cot, the one on the other side of Terry O'Reilly's, and dragged out a duffle bag. After unlacing it, he dug through clothes until he found a small blue jar. He held it out—Vicks VapoRub.

"I don't have a cold," Jason said.

"Smear a bit across your upper lip. Trust me, the menthol helps till you get used to it here. In a few days, you won't even notice the smell any longer."

Jason took it hesitantly, then unscrewed the lid and scooped out a small glob of gooey yellow-white ointment with his index finger. When Clay gestured for him to continue, he smeared it just under his nose. The sharp odor of menthol filled his nostrils and made his eyes water—but a second later, he realized he couldn't smell the room, or anything else, anymore.

"Hey—thanks!" Blinking hard to control watering eyes, he offered the jar back to Clay. "It works!"

"Keep it. The base doctor gave it to me on my first day here. I don't need it now."

Jason smiled. "Appreciate it."

"No problem, man."

Terry snorted, lowering his voice. "The three of us have to stick together. The army will close ranks and deny everything the moment we aren't useful anymore. Clay and I are geologists. Know why we're here?"

"I'd guess…something to do with the tunnel?"

"We're the ones who found the UFO. That's what it is, you

know—"

"We *don't* know that!" Clay said sharply.

"Get your head out of your ass, Clay!" Terry snapped. "We just found one of the crew!"

"Whoa!" Jason stared from one man to the other. "You found—"

"E.T. himself. Frozen in the ice like one of those wooly mammoths in Siberia."

"We *don't* know what it is," Clay said stubbornly. "The general says it's a sea lion."

"It's nothing from this planet," Terry said, lowering his voice to a whisper. "You *know* that, Clay. You saw it. You can't possibly buy Wu's bullshit story about it being a sea lion." He laughed, but it came out more like a crazy cackle. "No wonder we're all so goddamn messed up. You can't trust the military to tell the truth? Who would have thought!"

"Well, I know General Wu and Colonel Bloch both believe it's a spaceship," Jason said in a quiet voice. Was he breaking any confidences? After all, Terry knew—or had guessed—its origin already. And Clay couldn't be far behind. "That weird, super-light silver metal you found? It violates more rules of nature than I can count. It *can't* exist, and yet it does."

"Then the laws of nature are wrong," Clay said.

"More likely they can be bent," Jason said. He leaned forward. "We just don't know how yet. You ever hear of Clarke's Law?"

Clay looked blank.

"I think I know this one." Terry snapped his fingers. "Something about magic—"

"Sufficiently advanced technology is indistinguishable from magic," Jason said.

"Yeah! That's it!" He turned to Clay. "This sci-fi writer named Arthur C. Clarke thought it up. The *2001* guy. How would a jet airplane look to a neanderthal? Like magic. Smart guy, Clarke."

"Now," Jason said, "apply Clarke's Test to this metal. It doesn't look like magic to me—to any of us—right? Of course not. It's clearly science, just a science we haven't mastered yet. It's some kind of advanced metallurgy, a wacky alloy of aluminum or steel and exotic matter or God knows what. But it's been made by science. *Ipso facto*, since we recognize it as man-made—or alien-made in this case—

it's *not* that advanced. Maybe the beings who made it are fifty or a hundred or even a thousand years ahead of us. But not a hundred thousand years. *That* would look like magic. I'm betting it's closer to fifty years, myself, considering the speed at which our technology is advancing. We probably need a single breakthrough to explain it, maybe even replicate it, and then everything we've seen here will fall into place."

"Wow," said Clay, staring at him. "When you put it that way—"

"—suddenly it's not so scary," Terry finished. "But you didn't see that alien thing in the ice, Jase. God, it made my skin crawl!"

"Spiders do that for me," Jason said. He stifled another yawn. "I want to hit them with a shovel. Even though I know they're good for the environment and eat pests and all, I want them dead. I can't help myself." He shrugged. "It doesn't mean spiders are evil. Just different from us, and I'm hardwired to hate them. Maybe you're hardwired to hate whatever this thing is."

"You need to tell the soldiers that." Clay jerked his head toward the door. "Some of them got pretty freaked out. They're having a party in the rec room, but it's really gloomy, all things considered."

"Rain check." Jason rubbed at his eyes, which he suddenly realized had been burning for some time now. "It's been a long trip, and I'm crashing. I don't think I've slept more than a couple of hours in the last three days."

Clay nodded. "We were going to turn in, too. The army guys are all kids. I think the oldest is twenty-five. Little Energizer bunnies. They keep going and going and going. They'll be up for hours yet."

Terry added, "At least till the keg of beer runs out."

"We'll talk more in the morning, Jase." Clay stood and started unfastening the shoulder straps of his coveralls. Then he paused. "Do you play gin rummy, by any chance?"

CHAPTER 7

An old Joan Jett song blared from the jukebox in the rec room. A poker game at the table in the far corner occupied six men. The few others who hadn't turned in early clustered around the bar and the beer keg, talking in low voices. But the mood was anything but happy

Corporal Maria Menendez, dancing slowly by herself next to the jukebox, half a cup of beer in her left hand, kept an eye on them all. *Drinking—it's not just a job, it's a career.* She snorted, took another sip from her cup, and gave up the ghost of trying to party. Nobody was in the mood. Not even she herself.

That creature in the ice kept coming back to her. What was it? Not a sea lion, despite what the general had said. Maybe a dinosaur? The ice here was supposed to be millions of years old, after all. Yeah, that had to be it. Something older than humanity, something from the dawn of time, like in those old sci-fi movies her kid brother liked to watch.

Something smart.

Something that machined weird metal.

Something with red eyes...

Her cell phone gave a chainsaw buzz, and she pulled it out and held it up so the camera could recognize her face. A second later, the calendar popped open with the reminder she had set earlier: *CHANGE GUARD SHIFT.* Almost nine P.M. Time to relieve Dobbs. He would still have plenty of time to hang out with his bros.

She glanced around the room. *Who gets to relieve him?* A better question might be, *Who is the least drunk?*

The guys at the bar were more than halfway to shit-faced. Screw them. They'd just go down and fall asleep, maybe take a piss in a corner, and wouldn't that be something for the general to find in the morning? If she hadn't been driving the general's golf cart, she would have assigned shifts before she left. And if that dino-monster-creature hadn't thrown her off her game...

Yeah, it was the general's fault, really. But that was army life. No one here would have dreamed of messing with that creature. It didn't need to be guarded. What was Wu afraid of? That it would suddenly come alive and attack them? She snorted. This wasn't some Blumhouse movie.

Her gaze drifted to the poker players. Tim Seetoo? Yes, he was the quiet one, and from the looks of his cup—and the growing stack of cash in front of him—he'd barely had anything to drink. He could have the next shift.

With a tight smile, she crossed to the poker table, bent, and said, "Seetoo, I need you to relieve Dobbs and take the next shift. I'll have someone relieve you at midnight."

"Aw, Corporal," said Chuck Renner. The Texas twang grew more pronounced whenever he drank. "Don't take Seetoo now—he's winnin'."

"You want to be a winner, Renner? Congrats, you can have the midnight shift. I'll send your relief down at three a.m."

Chuckles came from the other four players, but none of them met her gaze. Clearly no one wanted the graveyard shift.

With a shrug and a lopsided grin, Seetoo scooped up the crinkled, well-worn bills in front of him and patted them into a neat stack.

"Have a heart, guys," he said. "I never win."

He pushed back his chair and stood, turning to her, "Want my lucky seat?"

"You know I don't gamble," Menendez said. She took a sip of her beer. "I don't take unnecessary risks with my money."

"We know, we know, still puttin' your brother through college." Kyle Kavanaugh regarded her with his heavy-lidded eyes.

She glanced across at him. "Then medical school. He's going to be a doctor. We have a plan."

"Your loss Corporal." Seetoo shoved the bills into his breast pocket and headed for the door. "You gotta have some fun. You only live once."

"Fun," she said. "Why not." She looked at the others seated at the table. "Let's play a game. Why don't you cut the cards?"

"Why?" Kavanaugh grinned up at her.

"High card gets three A.M. guard shift, low card gets six A.M. Fair enough?"

"Sure." He gave the deck a quick shuffle. His gaze never left her face.

He leaned forward and slapped the stack of cards down in front of her.

"You first?" he asked.

Everyone looked at her expectantly.

"Okay," she said. Had to be fair, after all. And with six people, odds were in her favor. It wasn't like money was involved.

She reached out, lifted the top quarter inch of the deck, and turned it over. Three of hearts. So much for odds. She showed everyone, then put the card back.

John Red Fox laughed. "Looks like you get dawn patrol," he said.

"We'll see."

Renner turned to the man to his right. "Foxy?"

Red Fox cut to the ten of spades. A solid middle card, likely safe. The next soldier got the eight of clubs, the next the six of clubs. Yerkins picked the Jack of diamonds.

"Shit," he said in a flat voice, and that got a laugh from everyone.

"Your turn, Kavanaugh," Menendez said.

With a bark of a laugh, he lifted a stack of cards, tilted it toward himself, and stared. His expression remained blank.

"Well?" said Yerkins. "Did you beat me?"

"Nope." He tossed the card face-up onto the table. "Deuce of hearts. I get 6 A.M."

CHAPTER 8

At one minute before nine P.M., Tim Seetoo strolled down the ice tunnel, listening to the whir of ventilator fans. A chill started to seep through his clothes. Thank God it was only three hours. At least it would be three hours well spent working on his novel, even if he did have to dictate it into his phone. The real-life story of a Japanese kid who enlisted in the army only to find himself helping to dig up a UFO in Antarctica would be a guaranteed best-seller. A million-dollar movie sale, too. Abso-tively guaranteed.

He rounded the final switchback and spotted Dobbs slouched forward in the driver's seat of the nearest mini bulldozer, half in shadow. Dobbs' eyes seemed to glint red for an instant, then he raised his head an inch, as though just awakening from a nap. He had a woozy, out-of-it stare. Doped up? Wouldn't be the first time…though Seetoo had figured his stashes would have run out long before now. Not like you could call your dealer for a delivery out here.

"You are relieved," Seetoo said. Best to stick to formalities. "Status report?"

"Situation…normal. Nothing…to report."

When Dobbs sat up, Seetoo noticed dark stains all over the front of his shirt. Vomit? Then, as Dobbs climbed down from the cab, half swaying, Seetoo noticed how the stains extended down the front of his pants, too, nearly to the knees. Not vomit, either. Too dark. Blood?

"What happened?" he demanded. "You okay?"

"What?" Dobbs snapped his head around, and his eyes suddenly focused, as though seeing him for the first time.

"You're covered in blood." Seetoo gestured. "Did you cut yourself on a piece of ice?"

"Huh?" Dobbs looked down. "Oh…it was just a nosebleed. It's…too dry…down here."

Seetoo looked at the tunnel walls. "Yeah, surrounded by a frozen ocean, and it's too dry." He laughed. "Better get a drink before the keg runs out. But you might want to get cleaned up first. And maybe see the doc about that nosebleed."

"Yeah…good idea. I'll…do that." Dobbs forced a smile. Catch you…soon."

Swaying slightly, he started up the tunnel.

Eyes narrowing, Seetoo turned to watch him. Dobbs' stride grew faster and more confident as he went, and by the time he reached the first switchback, he made the turn swiftly. He vanished from sight without a backward glance.

"Definitely high," Seetoo muttered to himself. A nosebleed from the dryness? More likely he'd found some coke and snorted it.

He started to slip into the seat of the mini bulldozer, noticed it was covered with blood, and stopped. When he got back up to the base, he'd report it to Menendez and let it be her problem. He wasn't going to clean up after Dobbs.

He went to the front of the 'dozer. The shovel had been lowered to the ground, and he perched on it while he unbuttoned his jacket's breast pocket and dug out his phone. With practiced ease, he thumbed it on. Sixty-two percent power. Enough to get a dozen pages in.

He opened Dictator One, his voice dictation software, and selected New File. After tapping the microphone icon, he opened his mouth and began: "Chapter Nine. In the tunnel."

Then a heavy hand fell on his shoulder, and he yelped in surprise.

Scrambling to his feet, he dropped his phone and whirled.

He half expected guffaws from Kavanaugh or one of the other guys. They seemed to get a special jolt of pleasure every time they pranked him. But it was Dobbs—stark naked, standing barefoot on the ice, and swaying as if about to fall.

"What the hell?" Seetoo said. He looked up the tunnel. "How did you get back here—I just saw you leave!"

Dobbs—the Dobbs in uniform—had vanished from sight. Had he doubled back? And where were his clothes?

"That—wasn't—me," the naked Dobbs gasped. He took a step, stumbled, fell forward.

Without a second's thought, Seetoo leaped to catch him.

Only it wasn't like catching flesh and bone. Seetoo's hands went wrist-deep into Dobbs' chest, as though plunged into a tub of gelatin. Seetoo looked down. Warm flesh oozed up over his forearms, then up to his elbows, like a thick sludge. This skin prickled, then began to burn.

"Let—me—go!" he cried, and that sounded stupid, even to him. He tried to jump back, but Dobbs's legs were melting over his shoes. Then the man's face began to twist, to distort, the mouth gaping wide—wider—impossibly wide—still stretching—

Sleep... he heard a voice in his head say.

"*No!*" he cried.

He jerked like a fish on a line. For a second, he had his right arm free. It was red and bloody, the skin stripped off like the bark of a tree. He backed up, pulling one foot loose, and thought he might tear away. But then he looked up into that mouth, now bristling with row after row of needle-like teeth. It gaped wider by the second.

Sleep... said the voice.

Wide enough now to swallow his head, that maw lashed forward—

Sleep...

He tried to scream, but darkness took him.

CHAPTER 9

General Wu sat at his tiny desk in the tiny office adjacent to his bedroom and watched a live feed playing from Space Station 5. NASA's climate-change monitoring space station had picked up a crude transmission in Morse code from Mars two hours ago, and if another message came through, they would have it first—at least until their orbit took them out of range. Then it would be Space Station 4's turn.

The stranded Mars expedition had finally made contact, though their brief message was puzzling: ALIVE SEND SEEDS ALIVE SEND SEEDS. It had repeated over and over for almost an hour before cutting out. No news about survivors. No news about his daughter.

Send seeds? Had something happened to their hydroponics equipment? His imagination leapt to cataclysmic failures of a dozen kinds. Was everyone there now starving to death? Or were they simply growing bored with beans and tomatoes?

They had brought, according to the people who knew the mission's inventory, seed stocks for a dozen different species of vegetable plants, with the hopes that something would grow well in the lesser gravity and diminished sunlight of Mars. The Earth plants were supposed to supplement the food they had brought with them, but with the destruction of the relief ship, who knew the state of their supplies?

And what seeds did they want? Would NASA be able to send them safely? And how long would it take to get a new supply ship to Mars?

Discussions had exploded on the Pentagon's live chat, but he had chosen to lurk in the background this time. It wasn't his project, after all. What could he possibly contribute from Antarctica? So he sat back and soaked up the opinions and speculations rattled off by everyone in the space program who thought they knew best.

The consensus seemed promising, though. He knew a relief rocket was under construction—fast-tracked when the last resupply ship exploded just before setting down—and everyone on the live chat seemed to agree that dropping a few pounds of survival gear in favor of seeds, and perhaps some spores for edible mushrooms like portabellas, would be a good trade-off.

He stifled a yawn and glanced at the laptop's clock. Only 21:37, but it felt like midnight. *I must be getting old*, he thought.

He shut the laptop's lid with a snap. Let those in the space program sort it out. His daughter would be fine. Karen had been on the ground when the relief ship exploded—she had to be one of the survivors.

Right now, he had more immediate problems. Problems he could actually do something about.

He was rising to head for his bedroom and some much-needed sleep when a couple of light, hesitant taps sounded on the door. Bloch, no doubt, with his usual inopportune timing.

"Come in," he called.

The handle turned and the door opened slowly. Instead of Colonel Bloch, Private Dobbs stood there, looking freshly showered and bright eyed. Great. The biggest basket case on the team. Wu stifled a yawn and kept his face impassive.

"Sir," Dobbs said, saluting.

"What is it, Private?" He returned the salute.

"Do you have a minute, sir? It's about that…uh…thing we found. In the ice."

"The sea lion." Wu rubbed his eyes. "Can it wait till morning? You should be having a drink with the rest of the team. Know when it's time to celebrate, son."

Dobbs smiled and stepped forward.

Then, behind Dobbs, Bloch appeared as if on cue. *Saved.* Wu leaned back in his chair and laced his fingers across his stomach.

"Unless it's life or death, Private," he said, "I'm afraid it will have to wait till morning." He jerked his chin toward Bloch. "No time right now. Dismissed."

Dobbs turned and noted Bloch's arrival for the first time. "Yes sir," he said. "It can wait." With another salute, he hurried back into the hall, turned, and headed back toward the rec room.

Wu waved Bloch inside. The colonel entered and closed the door.

"Anything I need to know about Dobbs, sir?" Bloch asked, staring after the man.

"I doubt it." Wu made a dismissive gesture. "He said he wanted to talk about the thing in the ice. Want to bet it freaked him out, and now he's angling to get shipped back home?" He chuckled. "That's the price you pay for having an open-door policy. Sometimes people take you up on it." He didn't add, *Like you. Like now. When I only want to get to sleep.* "What's up?"

"The Mars expedition," Bloch began. "Were you invited to the live chat—?"

Wu nodded. "I just got off."

"Any news about your daughter?"

"No, but if anyone's going to make it back to Earth, it will be her." Might as well make the most of having Bloch here. He waved the colonel to a chair. "Tell me about Cosgrove. How is he settling in?"

Bloch sat slowly, leaning forward and tucking his hands between his knees. Wu recognized it as a stalling technique. Was something wrong?

"I believe," Bloch began slowly, "that he is a better fit for us than Dr. Oud—or will be in the long run. He's still quite angry about being strong-armed into joining the team, but his interest in the metal clearly outweighs everything else. Where Dr. Oud focused on trying to understand the science behind the metal, Dr. Cosgrove is already looking ahead to its practical applications. He expects to understand it eventually."

"Sounds promising." It would have been the best news of the day, if not for the space station picking up a message from Mars.

"And he seems more stable than Dr. Oud was. Grounded, perhaps, with something to focus on that isn't just here."

"You mean his asteroid mining project?"

"Yes, sir."

Wu shifted. "Why do I hear a 'but' in there somewhere?"

"Sir, I can't quite say why, but something strikes me as slightly off about him. I wish we'd had time to get a psychological write-up done. He checks all the boxes, but something feels wrong."

"Elaborate."

Bloch shifted in his seat and looked uncomfortable. "It's just a feeling. I can't quite explain it." He shrugged vaguely. "I know he's saying the right things and doing the right things so far. But he's only saying and doing what we expect—going through the motions, playing along. While all the time he's planning to stab us in the back at the first opportunity."

Paranoid much, Colonel? That hadn't been his read on Cosgrove at all—not by a long shot. If anything, Cosgrove struck him as an idealist trying to do the best for mankind. Wu looked away, frowning. Could he have misread the man? Or was Bloch going off the deep end? *This place does get under your skin...* He'd need to keep an eye on them both.

After a heartbeat, he said, "I had hoped Dr. Cosgrove would be a smooth fit with the team. But if you suspect problems, we will need to monitor his actions."

"Thank you, sir." Bloch exhaled and seemed to relax.

He was holding his breath waiting for my answer, Wu thought. *Like he thought I'd disagree.*

Wu asked, "Do you have any recommendations?"

"Not yet, sir."

"Mm." He nodded. "Off the cuff, it occurs to me that it might be useful to assign him an assistant."

"To watch and report back?" Bloch asked.

"Exactly. I was thinking of Zielinski."

Bloch raised his eyebrows. "He's still in the infirmary, isn't he?"

"Doc says he can return to light duty tomorrow." *Not even putting a pickaxe through your calf can save you here,* Wu thought. The doctor half believed Zielinski did it on purpose, but he had no way to prove it short of a confession. And Zielinski insisted his hand slipped. *Accidents do happen.* Especially with the level of strain his people were under. They were lucky more accidents hadn't happened.

"Good news, then."

"Doc updated me a couple of hours ago. Zielinski is up on crutches. One more night under observation in the infirmary, then he'll be released. He won't be fit to work in the tunnel for at least six weeks, maybe a bit longer. Light duty. I was going to assign him to help Cookie, but this will be better. Keep his mind busy. And it won't pull an able-bodied man from work in the tunnel."

"Excellent idea, sir." Bloch pulled a little notebook from his shirt pocket, scribbled a quick note with a pencil, then tucked the book away. "I'll take care of it first thing tomorrow, after breakfast."

"Good. Now—what about the men? Any issues with today's discovery?"

"Nothing I've noticed, sir. I spent half an hour in the rec room while they celebrated. Of course, I heard some wild speculation about the creature in the ice—"

"To be expected," Wu said.

"—but they dropped it pretty quickly. And tomorrow news of the Mars expedition's message will be public, so that will also be a distraction. Corporal Menendez filed her daily report, and she doesn't mention anything unusual, beyond the finds in the tunnel. So, good news all around."

Wu nodded. Yes, good news indeed, despite Bloch's unease about Cosgrove. But then the colonel always had been a glass half-empty man.

"One issue," and Bloch cleared his throat, "is that Dr. Cosgrove has already requested a scanning electron microscope."

"He needs the tools of his trade. I understand."

"I'm worried about the red flags it might raise with the budget office."

"Keep trying. I know, I know—we don't need bureaucrats questioning why we need a scanning electron microscope at a meteor impact site. But the Mars expedition is going to be a distraction for the next few days, so this might be the best time to act. If you can get it without attracting undue attention, proceed. If not…"

"Understood, sir."

"Anything else?"

"No, sir."

Wu stood. "Then that will be all. Dismissed."

CHAPTER 10

"Hey, Dobbs," Yerkins called. He tossed his phone onto the blanket at the foot of his bed as Dobbs strolled into the dormitory.

"Hey," Dobbs said.

"You missed an epic poker game. Seetoo just about cleaned me out, if you can believe it. Then Kavanaugh finished me off."

"Ha. That's because you play like my grandmother. Game still going on?"

Yerkins shrugged. "Must be. But I'm tapped."

"Want me to spot you fifty till payday?"

"Sure, if you're willing." Yerkins grinned. "Still can't believe I lost to *Seetoo*. Beginner's luck, if you ask me." Then he squinted up at Dobbs. Why would *he* loan out cash? Dobbs never stuck his neck out for anyone.

"Happy to help." Then Dobbs added, as if reading his mind: "But you'll have to take my guard shift next time Menendez sticks me down there."

"Yeah." Yerkins pulled a sour face. A guard shift—of course there was an ulterior move.

Dobbs gave a visible shiver. "Damn thing in the ice freaks me out, you know?"

"Me too. That red eye…"

Then Dobbs brightened a little. "Anyway. It looks like Seetoo's luck has turned. He took a bad fall in the tunnel."

"Is he okay?"

"Banged his nose and bled like hell for a few minutes." Dobbs shrugged. "Asked me to get him some clean coveralls. He's soaked in blood."

He crossed to Seetoo's trunk, swung open the lid, and pulled out spare clothing. "Back in a minute." He started for the door.

"I'll save you a seat."

* * * *

Yerkins had no trouble buying back into the poker game using promised credit from Dobbs. Everyone knew Dobbs was good for it; he'd been the big winner the last time they played, and—obnoxious prick that he was—he'd crowed about it for the next three days. As he had no way to blow the cash on smokes or drugs or booze out here, of course he still had it.

So the other five players had each kicked in ten bucks for Yerkins. To their consternation—and Yerk's glee—he proceeded to win the next two hands with a full house, then an eight-high straight. By a rough reckoning, that put him up nearly forty dollars already. You could only win so much with the group's three-dollar limit on raises, but it was a friendly game, and low stakes were meant to keep players in as long as possible.

"Here's your sugar-daddy, Yerk," Chuck Renner said, waving a thumb toward the door.

It had been about ten minutes since Yerkins had joined the game, time enough for four hands.

Yerkins glanced down at his cards—utter garbage—and said, "I fold." He tossed them into the center of the table.

Then, glancing toward the door, he spotted Dobbs. The man stood just outside, looking over the room. His gaze drifted from the bar to the poker players, and then their eyes locked for a second. Dobbs smiled, but it seemed more coldly calculating than anything else. But that was just Dobbs being Dobbs.

Yerkins waved and turned back to the game. Chuck fanned his cards across the tabletop.

"Two pair," he said smugly. "Kings and Jacks."

Groans came from everyone still playing. They threw down their hands, and as Chuck raked in his winnings with a smug grin, Kavanaugh shuffled quickly.

"Five card draw," he announced. He began to deal. "Nothing wild, jacks or better to open."

Another bad hand. Yerkins skipped the first betting round and folded. Where was Dobbs?

He glanced around and spotted Dobbs helping himself to beer at the bar. He filled a plastic cup, steered around Corporal Menendez—dancing by herself beside the jukebox as The Pretenders played—and came over to the poker table, where he took up a position behind

D.C. Wilson.

"Aces over jacks," Kavanaugh announced, laying his cards face-up one by one.

Everyone still in the game tossed down their cards with new groans of disgust. Kavanaugh raked in the cash, as the deal passed to Red Fox. As Red began to shuffle, Yerkins tossed his dollar ante into the pot, and the others did the same.

Dobbs stared down at the table like he'd never seen poker before.

"I saved you a seat, Dobbs." Yerkins gestured to the empty chair at his right. "You gonna play or what?"

"Thanks." Dobbs rounded the table, slid into the chair.

Kavanaugh smirked. "Yerk says you're stakin' him for fifty, so we advanced it. No harm done, right, Dobbs?"

"No worries."' Dobbs pulled out a roll of bills and slowly peeled off ten fives. When he tossed them into the middle of the table, the other players retrieved their shares. Then Dobbs put a dollar into the pot for his own ante.

"I appreciate it, Dobbs," said Yerkins.

"You know I got your back."

Yeah, Yerkins thought, *and I got your next guard shift.*

Red Fox said, "Five card stud, one up, three down, one up." He began to deal.

Kavanaugh looked over at Dobbs. "Seetoo okay?" he asked. "Yerk said something about him busting his nose?"

Dobbs shrugged. "Nah, it's not broken, just a bleeder. He's already forgotten about it. Back to work on his novel."

The whole table laughed.

"His novel?" said Yerkins. Why was he always the last to know?

"Hell," Chuck Renner drawled, leaning back in his chair, "if he's gonna be a famous author, I'm gonna be the goddamn Pope!"

"He let me see a few chapters last week," Red Fox said slowly, face serious. "It's pretty good, actually. The guy can write. You know he sold a half dozen short stories to sci-fi magazines?"

"No shit?" said Renner.

"What's the novel about?" Yerkins asked.

"A soldier who gets sent to Antarctica and finds a UFO buried in the ice."

Everyone laughed again.

"Figures," Chuck Renner said. "We do all the work, he gets all the fame."

"Cut 'em." Red Fox set down the deck of cards. Kavanaugh cut them. "Did everyone ante? Pot looks right to me."

He began to deal.

"His book's about a UFO?" Yerkins turned the idea over in his head. "Like maybe we got here?" Was Red Fox pulling his leg?

Sounds like he's pullin' your leg," Renner said.

"Heaven's truth," said Red Fox, pausing to put a hand over his heart. "But he's wasting his time. No way is that book getting published. No way, not ever."

"Why?" Dobbs asked.

Chuck Renner leaned back in his chair. "Hell, boy, do we have to spell it out for you? You really think the government's gonna let some book about all the top-secret shit we got goin' on here ever get published?"

"Free speech, man!" said D.C Wilson. "How can they stop him?"

"Oh, they'll stop him," said Red Fox, scowling. "The men in black will show up and take him away. And his manuscript, too. We will never see either one again."

"Sounds like some kinda bad sci-fi movie," Kavanaugh said. "Come on, you're the opener, Dobbs. Let's play."

Dobbs looked at his cards. "Check."

Yerkins picked up his hand. Two jacks, two fours, an ace. Not bad. He could probably win without drawing another card. But he didn't want to tip his advantage too early. He checked, too, and the opening bet passed to his left.

"What do you mean, it sounds like a bad movie?" said Wilson. He rearranged his cards, frowned at them. "It would be an awesome movie. Seetoo better get someone good to play me, though. I'm holding out for the Rock. Or maybe Vin Diesel." He paused. "This hand sucks. Check."

"If he bases a character on me, I'm gonna sue," said Kavanaugh. He peered at them from under heavy eyelids. "He can't do that, can he? What do you think, Foxy?"

"I think I open for two dollars," Red Fox said. He tossed a pair of bills into the center of the table.

Betting continued around the table until it reached Dobbs, who raised his head and slowly looked around the circle of players. He paused when he got to Yerkins.

Yerk stared back impassively. No way was he giving this hand away.

But Dobbs said, "I fold." He dropped his cards face-down on the table.

* * * *

Midnight neared. Ten minutes before his guard shift, Chuck Renner stretched and announced, "That's it for me." He grabbed the few bills still remaining before him and stuffed them into his billfold. "Nice run of luck, Dobbs. But it ain't gonna last. Clean 'im out, Foxy. Catch y'all on the downside."

He headed for the door, pausing only long enough to grab a last beer for the road—or the tunnel in this case.

With a touch of envy, Yerkins studied the cash that had accumulated in front of Dobbs. Over the last two and a half hours, Dobbs had won steadily. He must have two or three hundred bucks by now.

Yerkins glanced down at his own meager stake—down to nineteen dollars. Enough for three or four more hands, if he played carefully. But with the way his luck had been running…

"I'm going to call it quits, too," he said, shoving back his chair and standing. Better to leave while he still had some money left to get into tomorrow night's game. His luck was bound to change by then. If not, Friday was payday. He could start over again.

"Don't forget, you owe me fifty," Dobbs reminded him.

He nodded, pocketing his cash. "Yeah, I know. I'll get it to you Friday. Thanks for the loan, Dobbs."

When he turned, he found the rest of the room had cleared out. Despite the keg of beer, no one must have really been in the mood to celebrate. Even Corporal Menendez, who closed every bar she went to, had given up the ghost early.

"Last hand," Kavanaugh announced. "Five card draw. Jacks or better to open. Progressive."

Yerkins started for the door. Behind him, he heard cards being dealt.

* * * *

After hitting the head, Yerkins brushed his teeth, scrubbed his face with a dribble of tepid water from one of the low-flow sinks, and walked as softly as he could into the darkened barracks. His was the third cot on the left wall. It groaned slightly as he sat and pulled off his shoes, then his shirt and pants. He folded everything and put it into his trunk. Around him, he noticed a couple of dim glows from cell phones, heard the sounds of more than a dozen men already asleep, or nearly so. The soft snores, the raspy breaths, the dream-mutterings and whimpers and soft cries that marked the nightmares plaguing them all—it provided a familiar background noise.

He pulled his phone from his pants pocket, plugged it in, and set its alarm for 02:50. Menendez would skin him alive if he missed his shift guarding the "sea lion" in the ice. Then he slid the phone under his pillow. It should be loud enough to wake him, but hopefully not loud enough to bother anyone else in the room.

Lying down, he pulled up his sheet and blanket. Through half closed eyes, he saw Red Fox and the poker players trickle in one by one to find their beds and collapse.

To his left, a sleeper cried out softly, *"N-o-o-o—"* before subsiding with a moan.

Everyone had now returned from the poker game except Dobbs. Where was he? Yerkins found himself abruptly wide awake. It was like waiting for a shoe to drop.

Then exhaustion washed over him. He closed his eyes, and he slept, and he dreamed, and in his dream strange, cold, three-fingered hands reached for him out of the darkness.

Softly, he began to whimper.

CHAPTER 11

Specialist Audrey Petersen, bulky earphones covering her ears, head cocked slightly to one side, listened with eyes closed. The base radio, a Codan 2140Q, a dual-mode HF and UHF set, was the most beautiful thing in the world, as far as she was concerned. As she eavesdropped on the sounds of the universe, the faint shush of background noise, the bleeps of white noise from solar flares, her fingers slowly turned the frequency dial. Of course, the computer could scan just as well as she could, but she loved the feel of the controls under her fingertips, as she finessed each frequency in search of anything unusual.

A few snatches of what might have been Russian broke through. With her free hand, she jabbed RECORD on the array. She lingered on that frequency, straining to hear.

"*Da,*" a voice said distinctly. There was a burst of static, then what sounded like: "*Tvoya sestra nosit armeyskiye sapogi.*" More static. "*Vorona letit v polnoch.*" Then: "*Sosud s pestikom soderzhit nastoyashchiy napitok.*" Dead air followed. Ten seconds, twenty.

Definitely something. She stopped the recording, exported it as an .mp3 file, and added it to the queue for the hourly satellite upload to the C.I.A. station in Punta Arenas, Chile. Then she picked up the clipboard, glanced at the clock on the wall, and logged the time and the radio frequency. Let the analysts back home figure it out. They were lucky she'd caught it.

She jumped as warm hands fell on her shoulders. Spinning her chair around, she found Dobbs standing behind her with a distant expression on his face. With the headphones on, she hadn't heard him come in.

He mouthed something.

"Wait," she said. She took off the headphones. "Now I can hear you."

"Just saying you look sexy tonight."

Petersen blushed, looked away. "I bet you say that to all the radio geeks." She tucked a stray lock of hair behind her left ear.

He laughed. "No, really. You get this dreamy, far-away look when you're on the radio. And this monster—" He gestured at the four-foot-tall array of equipment on the desk in front of her. "How can I hope to compete?"

They'd had an on-again, off-again relationship for a few years. Currently it was off, but…it wasn't like she'd found somebody new. And from the look of things, he hadn't, either. Not that they had much choice out here.

"What are you doing here?" she asked. "Can't sleep?"

He made a face. "Menendez stuck me on guard duty. Not that there's anything worth guarding. My shift ended, but I'm still amped, so I thought I'd come by and see what you're up to."

She leaned back and glanced up at the clock. "I'm on duty for another forty-five minutes. If you can stay awake, come back and we'll get coffee in the mess. Chat a bit."

"Like old times?"

"Yeah."

"Better idea. You keep scanning, and I'll rub your shoulders." He grinned. "After that…"

"After that, I'm going to bed."

"Yeah. If that's what you want."

She remembered Dobbs's massage skills. She felt herself weakening. Her neck did ache… What could it hurt?

"Maybe—but only for a minute. I just caught a voice saying something in Russian. I don't want to miss it if they come on again.

"They're just messing with you. You know they'd scramble anything important."

"Maybe." She shrugged. "Remember the time they were trading insults with a Chinese general in English, because that was the only language they had in common?"

"Oh, yeah. You played it for me. Funny as hell."

"The joke was on me." She sighed. "General Wu heard it and got me added to his staff. Lucky me."

"Come on, turn around. No self-pity. I can tell your shoulders are tense."

"Okay. But only for a minute. And I have to keep listening."

"I won't stop you."

She pulled the headphones over her ears and turned back to the radio. Dobbs touched her shoulders gently, began to knead. She closed her eyes, leaning back slightly.

Damn it, that felt good. Why had she dumped him the last time? Her thoughts were growing fuzzy.

Warmth spread to her neck, then to her arms, as though she were slowly settling into a blood-warm bath.

Sleep...

Her eyes fluttered. No. She couldn't sleep. She could be written up if she fell asleep on duty!

Sleep...

It was like struggling up through a bottomless pool of warm syrup. She opened her mouth to gasp, and something moist and warm filled it.

Her arms jerked, and she lost her grip on the frequency dial.

Sleep...

Somehow, her eyes opened. Something wet and sticky clung to them—it was all over her face—dark and warm and moist and pulsating—

Pulsating?

What was happening?

She tried to thrash her way free. The earphones came off. Wet filled her ears. She couldn't see, couldn't hear.

Her arms jerked. Her legs spasmed.

Sleep...

CHAPTER 12

Jason Cosgrove woke with a jerk, panic surging through him. *Where am I?* He sat up, arms flailing. He thrashed loose from his sheet and stared frantically around the dim room. His heart pounded in his chest. *Have to get away—*

No. No need to panic, it had just been a dream. Something chasing him. Not real.

It came back. *Antarctica.* That was reality. What was that old army slogan? *It's not just an adventure.* A nightmare, more like it.

Taking a deep breath, he began the calming exercise he'd been using since he was a teenager and first saw *Dune* on TV.

He told himself, *Fear is the mind-killer*. He blinked, tried to see through the dimness. *I have no fear, for fear is the little death that kills me over and over.* Pressing his eyes tight, he took another deep breath and exhaled slowly. He felt his heartbeat slowing. *Without fear, I die but once.*

It was a litany he'd repeated hundreds, perhaps thousands of times in high school, when he'd been the science geek of all science geeks. Who would have thought a school with only 550 students could produce so many bullies?

Those days were best forgotten. He shook his head, forced the memories down. This wasn't the time or place.

Another breath. Another.

He opened his eyes. The darkness wasn't absolute.

A blade of light from the hallway cut across the far side of the room, lending a dim illumination to everything. He looked around, taking in the rows of uneasily-sleeping men on their cots. Almost as one, they tossed and turned.

Somewhere to his right, a man rasped out, *"Don't—oh—oh—don't—"* in a throaty whisper before subsiding into unintelligible mutters.

Jason rubbed crusty eyes. His head throbbed, and he felt anything but rested. Yet he knew he wouldn't be able to get back to sleep again. Jet-lag? Had to be.

The guy in the next bed—the geologist, he suddenly recalled, the one named Terry O'Malley—twitched suddenly. Then his legs spasmed like a dog chasing a rabbit in its sleep. Or fleeing some night terror.

Jase became aware that almost all of the men around him were stirring as one. Sheets swished. Springs creaked. Another moan came from behind him.

Definitely weird.

Shivering, he sat up and swung bare feet to the cold tile floor. Coffee. That would help. And then he needed to read and annotate Pieter's journals. No doubt he'd missed a lot when he skimmed them in the helicopter.

He took a deep breath. What time was it?

He searched the room, found a dimly glowing digital clock set high on the far wall. Its numerals read 04:22. Military time, of course.

He retrieved yesterday's pants and shirt from the trunk at the foot of his bed, pulled them on, then slipped on his shoes. Stretching, he headed for the latrine—as Col. Bloch had called it—which was, conveniently, the next door down to the right. Coffee might be a top priority, if he could find the kitchen, but his bladder came first. And second had to be a shower. He reeked. Even over the stench of the base and what remained of the Vicks VapoRub, he could smell his own body odor.

He relieved himself at one of the steel urinals, then poked around the men's room, acquainting himself with the facilities. Across from the toilet stalls and urinals sat six small sinks, also steel. Spray deodorant, mouthwash, 3-ounce paper tumblers, and plastic bins filled with disposable razors sat on a shelf over the sinks. It seemed as though the army had thought of everything.

An open doorway at the back of the room led to showers. There, taped beside the doorway, its lettering starting to run from humidity, a wrinkled, hand-written sign read:

Conserve water.
Max 3 mins every other day.
NON-POTABLE. (Do not drink.)

Unlimited ice outside, and they rationed water? He shook his head. Or maybe that's where they got the water they used? Distantly, he recalled something about not drinking water from glaciers—silt trapped inside it caused acute cases of Montezuma's Revenge. Do not drink, indeed.

He stuck his head into the shower area, a white-tiled room with six nozzles hanging from the ceiling and wide steel grates in the floor for drains. A stack of clean towels sat on a wire rack by the doorway, next to a wheeled hamper for used towels. The far wall sported industrial-sized pump bottles of body wash and shampoo—not a bad setup, all things considered. He'd belonged to gyms with fewer amenities.

He stripped, left his clothes on hooks outside the shower and turned the single handle to start the water, adjusting it to HOT. Overhead, pipes gurgled, then a stream of water began to dribble out from one of the nozzles. He stuck his foot into the flow. Tepid, not hot. But warm enough he could tolerate it, at least. He'd half expected the nozzle to jet out water just this side of ice cubes.

Three minutes didn't seem nearly long enough, so he stepped fully into the flow and began to lather up as fast as he could. Something reddish-brown caught his eye as it swirled across the white floor tiles. He stepped back, staring. Was that blood? His eyes began to sting; he tried to wipe soap away, made it worse. Then a tuft of what might have been short brown hair, with a piece of white scalp still attached, circled once before disappearing through one of the slits in the drain.

Get a grip. He shuddered, pressed his eyes closed. God, this place was already starting to get to him. It had only been a day, and he was already imagining things. *Fear is the mind-killer.* His last girlfriend had been addicted to true crime TV shows, and maybe he'd watched one too many with her. *I have no fear, for fear is the little death that kills me over and over.* Murder in the shower at an army base in Antarctica? Fat chance.

He opened his eyes, rubbed them, looked down. Nothing there. Not a trace of blood. Of course he'd imagined it.

Get your head straight. This is serious. Nobody is dead.

If you murdered someone here, the whole base would know almost instantly. How could you hide it? Even if you dumped the corpse outside, behind the mounds of debris from the tunnel excavation, everyone would notice a missing soldier. Didn't they have daily roll-calls, or something? Or maybe they didn't bother out here, where nobody could go AWOL. It would be a days-long trek to get to the Amundsen-Scott Station on foot, and you'd freeze long before you made it. Unless you stole the helicopter…but you'd have to know how to fly it. Or did they have snowmobiles?

Crazy. I'm just going crazy.

Like Pieter.

* * * *

Just after five A.M., he made it to "Mess Hall" as the hand-written sign on the wall outside proclaimed it. A far sight from the cheerful dining area at the Amundsen-Scott Station, the army's mess hall had two rows of long, steel tables with thirty or forty uncomfortable-but-sturdy looking folding chairs set up around them. But it had one feature every other room he'd seen on the base lacked: windows.

Five thick glass panels offered a stunning panoramic view of a bleak, frozen wasteland. The sun was up, even though it was still early in the morning, and light flooded in. He hurried over and gazed out.

The view struck him as both alien and stunning, like something you'd find in *National Geographic* or *Nature*. The sun, a small orange ball, hung low in the sky. The glacier seemed to stretch to infinity. Here and there, small bumps and irregularities in its ice cast long shadows like fingers reaching toward him.

He turned his head slowly, trying to take it all in. Nothing moved. No birds, no animals. To the far left, maybe a hundred yards away, he spotted heaped-up mounds of rock and broken ice. That had to be the dump he'd spotted from the helicopter yesterday, where they put debris from the underground tunnel they were digging.

"Who are you?" a man's voice rumbled behind him.

He jumped and whirled around.

A short, slightly overweight man with almond-colored skin and a large beak of a nose stood in the doorway to the kitchen area. He wore a white bib apron and held a large metal spoon in one hand.

"Hi," Jase said. He gave an awkward smile. "Jason Cosgrove. Jase. The new metallurgist?"

"Ah." The man nodded like it all made sense. "I'm Vitas—Vitas

Varnas. I know it's a mouthful. Call me Cookie. Everyone does."

"Because you're the cook?"

"Pastry chef. I specialize in Italian butter cookies."

"Wait. What?" Jase blinked. *Pastry chef?*

The man snorted a laugh. "Joking. Of course, I'm the cook. Breakfast is 06:00. No special orders. They upset us." He waved the spoon as if in warning. "And no between-meals snacks."

"I just wanted coffee."

Cookie jerked a thumb toward the far wall. "Coffee maker is on the table. Pods next to it. Help yourself." He turned and shuffled into the kitchen.

"Thanks."

Turning back to the window, Jason admired the view for a few seconds more, then sighed and headed for the coffee maker. Caffeine *was* a necessity at this point.

Behind the counter, Ahmed—Cookie—was already at work, banging pots and pans and setting bowls and other things out on the prep area by the stove. Jason spotted a white plastic jar the size of a beer barrel labelled simply EGGS in bold black letters, and a slightly smaller one labelled GRITS. Instant food—just add water and heat?

"You know Yerk—Private Yerkins?" Cookie called to him.

Jase thought for a second. "No, sorry." He hadn't been introduced to anyone named Yerk or Yerkins yet.

He took his mug of coffee from the machine, added creamer and sugar, then sipped experimentally. Way too hot.

"Yerk is supposed to be on KP duty—that's kitchen patrol—helping me this morning," Cookie went on. "He should have been here half an hour ago." Frowning, he glanced at the door. "Probably overslept again—wouldn't be the first time. Nobody ever gets a good night's sleep here."

"I noticed." After last night, he could vouch first-hand for the effect this place had. "How early do you get up?"

"Three-thirty A.M. every day." He sounded almost proud of it. "In eighteen years, I have never missed a meal."

"Wow."

Cookie shrugged modestly. "I'm used to it. It's all routine now. Or would be, if not for that thrice-damned Yerkins." He glared toward the door again.

"Well, I can give you a hand, if you need it."

"You're hired." Cookie looked at him and gave a wicked grin. "Grab an apron, newbie." He waved a spatula to the right, where Jason noticed a wall-hook holding a selection of white aprons.

"Newbie?" Jason asked. He took a deep swallow of coffee. "I've been cooking my whole life."

"Hah! New to army life. The first rule here is—never volunteer for anything."

"But it's more fun to cook for others than for yourself. And I make a mean omelet, if I do say so."

"No omelets—they take way too long. We are cooking for thirty, so speed and efficiency are everything. I'm already behind schedule on prep, thanks to Yerk."

"Then maybe biscuits? I just need the oven preheated to 350 for those."

"I'll set it. It holds up to four trays at a time. The way these guys eat, three batches ought to do it."

Jason nodded. His mother's recipe usually made ten biscuits at a time—just a matter of scaling it up a bit.

"Just let me finish my coffee."

He drained the cup, tossed it in the bin, and headed for the aprons.

Cookie, under his breath, was muttering something about "skinning that damn Yerkins alive when he shows up."

CHAPTER 13

Nate Yerkins came awake with a gasp. Someone was looming over him. He scrambled up on his elbows and tried to get his eyes to focus.

It was Chuck Renner, he realized a second later, and the burly Texan looked mad enough to spit.

In a low voice, Renner said, "You forgot to relieve me last night, Yerk."

Yerkins glanced at the clock on the wall—05:31. The automatic lights had come on in the dormitory. Men were beginning to drag themselves up with groans and stretches. Only Renner was already showered and dressed.

"Shit." Yerkins ran fingers through his hair. "Must have slept through my alarm. God, I'm so sorry, Renner. Did you—?"

Chuck glanced around, then sat on the foot of the bed and lowered his voice. "Nah, I ain't gonna report you. It happens. I stood double duty. Luckily Kavanaugh relieved me early." He poked a finger into Yerkins' chest, punctuating each word. "But. You. Owe. Me."

"Anything, Renner. You know that."

"And ain't you on KP duty this mornin'? Cookie's gonna be on the warpath."

With a yelp, Yerkins leaped out of bed. "Shit, shit, shit. Gotta book. Sorry, Renner."

He ran for the shower.

* * * *

Ten minutes later, hair still dripping, Yerkins pounded down the hallway at full speed, shirt in hand and belt unbuckled and flapping. He made the mess hall in record time—but still nearly an hour late. Panting, he drew up short, shrugged his shirt on over his tee, and cinched his belt tight. Then he trotted into the dining area.

Cookie glanced over his shoulder from the stove, frowned hard, then turned back to stirring something in a large steel vat. Probably rehydrated eggs. They had them every breakfast, along with grits or oatmeal, and usually sausage or bacon.

"Sorry, Cookie—" he began.

"No whining, Yerk," Cookie called. "Lucky thing Jase covered for you. I won't have to write you up." He paused. "*This* time."

Yerkins shook his head. "Who? Jase—?"

"That would be me." A man stepped out of the storeroom holding a tub of flour. Middle height, dark brown hair, wire thin and with an intense gaze. He wore one of Cookie's aprons and sported a white paper cap. "You must be Private Yerkins?"

"Uh, yes."

The guy introduced himself as the base's new metallurgist. "I'd offer to shake hands," he said, "but I'm covered in flour." He held up white-dusted fingers. But his smile seemed friendly enough.

"What are you doing?" he asked.

"Making biscuits."

Cookie looked over at them. "I told him we don't have time for biscuits," he said with a shrug, "but he insisted."

"Drop biscuits are fast and easy." Jase laughed. "You'll see. Is the oven ready?"

"Just hit 350," Cookie said. "But first, I want you to taste this." With a small spoon, he scooped out some of his scrambled eggs and offered them to Jase. Jase blew on them, then gave them a try.

"Delicious!" he proclaimed. "Is that turmeric?"

Cookie grinned. "You, my new friend, have a great palate. These louts—" He gestured grandly with his giant stirring spoon, taking in the rest of the base. "—wouldn't notice if I served them dog food on day-old toast."

"Hey!" Yerkins said. "I'm standing right here!"

Cookie said, "You disagree, Yerk?" He pointed with his spoon, grinning like a madman. "You, with your advanced palate and vast experience with gourmet dining, can pick out a hint of turmeric artfully concealed behind six other spices?"

"Well. No." Licking his lips, he stared between the two. He'd never seen Cookie in such a good mood. Best not to argue. Instead, he asked, "What's turmeric?"

"Listen to the man!" Cookie said, turning to Jase and shaking his head sadly. "Do you see what I have to put up with every day?

'What's turmeric?' Pearls to swine. It's all pearls to swine."

Jase turned to Yerkins. "It's in the ginger family—it's used in a lot of Indian and Asian dishes. You'll like it." To Cookie, he said, "Go on, give him a taste."

Cookie rolled his eyes, but grabbed a clean tablespoon, scooped up more scrambled eggs, and passed them over.

Yerkins took it sniffed the eggs hesitantly. They smelled of something different and maybe a little bit sweet. Since both Jase and Cookie were staring at him, he swallowed hard, took a deep breath, and put it in his mouth.

For once, the eggs didn't taste over-salted. And there was a hint of something hot at the back of his tongue, a little peppery, but not quite. A little sweet, too. But it seemed to go with the eggs really well. He chewed, swallowed, and then met their gazes.

"Well?" Cookie prompted.

"Hey. This *is* better than usual!"

"See?" Jase said. "He did notice. Oh, do you have any rosemary?"

"Of course. Yerk, fetch it from the storeroom. It's on the right with the spices—the stuff in the clear glass jars."

"Right." Yerkins turned and trudged for the storeroom, grabbing one of the white aprons on the way. Rosemary? What the hell was that?

Behind him, Cookie proclaimed, "It's going to be a *very* good day!"

* * * *

It was 06:04 when the first few zombie-eyed soldiers wandered in for breakfast. Yerkins had been kicked out of the cooking area— Cookie and Jase seemed to be trying to out-do each other with their cooking, and he only got in the way—so he took up his usual post at the serving counter. As soldiers approached with trays, he spooned out plates of scrambled eggs, grits, and sausage. The rosemary biscuits proved an even bigger hit than he'd expected. Who'd have thought something that looked like broken pine needles could smell and taste so good?

Chuck Renner was the first to finish, but instead of adding his tray to the dirty-dishes rack, he strode toward the serving counter.

"Something wrong?" Yerkins asked. Hadn't he liked it?

"Hit me again, Yerk." Renner held out his tray, so Yerkins scooped up another portion and added it to his plate. Then Chuck reached over the counter and helped himself to a third biscuit.

"Best I've had since I was stationed in Atlanta." He took a big bite, not even bothering with butter or jelly.

Yerkins lowered his voice. "It's that new guy, Jase." He jerked his head toward where Cookie and Jase stood talking by the stove. "He likes to cook, can you believe it? So now he's Cookie's best friend. I think they're showing off for each other."

"Hell, boy, if he makes biscuits like this every day, he's gonna be my best friend, too. I reckon he's a metals guy, like Doc Oud?"

"Yeah. Weird old dude. Intense. But kinda cool."

Renner squinted over at Jason. "Can't be more'n thirty-five, forty max. He ain't that old."

"Yeah. Whatever. Hey, can you run a tray down to Kavanaugh when you're done?"

"Ain't you supposed to do that?"

"Yeah, but I think everyone's going to be coming back for seconds today. We haven't had a meal this good since Easter."

Renner shrugged. "Sure, I guess even Kavanaugh's gotta eat." He lowered his voice. "But slip me another one of them biscuits first."

"Thank you." Yerkins added yet another biscuit to Renner's plate.

Renner leaned forward and called, "Hey Cookie! Great food today. Thanks. You too, new fella. Nice biscuits. Nearly as good as my mama's, and that's sayin' somethin'."

* * * *

Yerkins peeked into the officer's mess—the small conference room next door to the mess hall—for a head count and only found Colonel Bloch and General Wu seated at the table. Bloch and Wu always ate together there. Sometimes—usually when he needed something—Lieutenant Osprey would join. He was the base doctor. Usually, though, the doc got his own tray and ate in the infirmary.

Today was no different, just the two officers.

Promptly at 07:00, Yerkins put together trays for both men. Jase had just dumped another batch of twenty biscuits into the serving tray, so he snagged two for each officer, then hustled next door while the food was still hot.

Both Bloch and Wu shoved aside their laptops when he entered, and he slid trays in front of each of them. Then he came to attention and saluted.

"At ease, Private," the general said. He picked up a biscuit, sniffed it almost suspiciously. "Something new?"

"Rosemary biscuits, sir," Yerkins said, "the new guy—uh, Jase—he made them."

The general grunted. Was that approval?

"Dismissed."

CHAPTER 14

That had to be one of the best meals I've ever had on an army base, Col. Bloch thought, loosening his belt a notch as he turned right and headed for the infirmary. *And that includes Fort Jackson.* He'd been stationed at the South Carolina army base for a year, and he'd eaten some of the best barbecue and southern cooking of his life in their mess hall.

He still couldn't believe Dr. Cosgrove had made those biscuits. When the general joked, "Fuck science, let's keep him on as cook," Bloch had laughed and agreed. Cookie, though, had more than risen to the challenge—everything else had been above par, too. *Nothing like a little competition.*

It was almost enough to make him feel guilty about his suspicions of Jason. Anyone who baked like that couldn't be so bad…. could they?

He strode briskly down the corridor. The infirmary was a bare-bones affair, a twelve-foot by fifteen-foot room crammed to overflowing with an oversized desk, three beds separated by privacy curtains, a pair of medical supply cabinets, and a small refrigerator. It lay at the very end of the hallway.

The sign taped next to the door said, "Base Hospital" with either sarcasm or hopeful exuberance. Probably sarcasm, knowing the soldiers. He didn't know who put up all these signs, but he suspected Private Seetoo. Not that it had been bad for morale or anything. If anything, the men needed a little fun here.

Bloch glanced at his watch: 07:51. Then he paused, hand on the door handle.

Dr. Osprey normally kept the door open. Did he need privacy for some reason? Unless something had happened during the night—or everyone had suddenly come down with food poisoning from breakfast—Private Zielinski should be the only patient.

Best to be respectful of the doctor's domain. Bloch rapped sharply on the door, waited a couple of heartbeats for a reply, then knocked again. No answer came. Odd. Had the doctor stepped out? Maybe he had joined the men for breakfast in the mess hall.

Turning the handle, he pushed hard, half expecting it to be locked. The doctor always kept it locked when he wasn't there—light-fingered soldiers had been known to rifle the drug cabinet, if the opportunity presented itself. But today the door swung open easily. Bloch stepped inside, glancing around. The lights were on. Someone *ought* to be here.

The privacy curtain had been drawn around the middle bed where he'd last seen Zielinski lying. Through the semi-opaque wall of cloth, movement caught his eye—and then he heard a coughing, retching sound. Vomiting? He frowned. You didn't throw up from putting a pick-axe through your leg.

"Everything okay?" he called. He took a half step forward. If it was a medical emergency, he didn't want to intrude. "Doc?"

No answer.

"Doctor Osprey?"

No answer. Another retching, gasping wheeze came, then the violent sound of uncontrollable vomiting. Movement on the floor drew his eye. A pool of dark red liquid slowly pushed out from behind the curtain.

What the hell? Bloch stared down at the blood for a second. Then he sprang forward and yanked back the privacy curtain. It hissed open on its rollers.

The doctor—face blotchy and blood-smeared, medical coat now more crimson than white—lay on the cot. He twitched, hands knotting into fists, and then his back arched in agony. Spasms wracked his body As the spasms passed, he sank down with a wheezing, gasping whimper. A bubble of blood formed at his mouth. Popped.

Next to the bed, dressed only in his skivvies and standing on crutches, stood Private Zielinski. Bloch noted, almost in passing, a large white bandage on the man's left calf. Zielinski seemed frozen in place—staring down at the doctor with his mouth gaping and an expression that could only be described as horrified. *Useless.*

"Doc—" Bloch said. He leaped forward and grabbed the lieutenant's shoulder, rolled him onto his side. Didn't that let people breathe easier? Help clear their airway?

The doctor moaned. Then his eyes rolled up, showing all white.

His back arched again as he went rigid with pain.

"Easy, easy," Bloch whispered, voice as soothing as he could make it. "Try to relax. Try to breathe. What—what can I do to help?"

The doctor choked, wheezed. He didn't seem able to speak. His eyes stayed rolled up, the whites shot through with thick red lines. A bubbling sound came from his chest. *Something in his lungs, maybe?*

Bloch glanced up at Zielinski. "What happened?"

The private stared blankly at him.

"What happened?" Bloch bellowed.

The private seemed to shake himself back to alertness.

"Sir—uh—sir—he was helping me onto my crutches. But then he started coughing up blood. I—I didn't know what to do! He— he just fell over on the bed—and then he started shaking! And the blood— What—do you know what's wrong with him?"

Bloch looked down. The doctor wheezed one last time, jerked violently, lay still. His head slowly settled to one side, almost like a balloon deflating. A trickle of blood ran from the corner of his mouth onto the pillow.

Dead? Tentatively, Bloch reached out and touched the man's neck, checking for a pulse. Nothing.

He met Zielinski's gaze. Zielinski's eyes were huge, round—terrified.

So much blood.

"Wait here," Bloch said. Somehow, he managed to keep his voice under control. "Stand at the door and don't let anyone in till I get back."

The general had to be informed.

Without waiting for an answer, he turned and strode to the corridor, paused, peeked out. Fifty feet away, Corporal Menendez exited the mess hall with two other soldiers. Laughing and talking, they turned and strolled in the other direction, toward the dormitory building. They didn't even glance toward the infirmary.

Bloch counted to ten, then forced himself to walk after them at a normal pace. His heart pounded and he heard a roaring in his ears loud enough to wake the dead. *I can't believe the doctor's gone.* When he reached the mess hall's open doorway, he kept going without even a glance inside.

Suddenly he was at the officers' dining room. He slipped inside, closed the door behind himself, and sank back against it.

Fortunately, General Wu hadn't left yet. The general had shoved aside his tray and returned to his laptop, reviewing what looked like a new Mars report. Of course, with his daughter stranded there, who could blame him?

Wu glanced up and seemed to read the expression on his face.

"What's wrong?" he demanded. He shut his laptop's lid with an audible snap.

Bloch swallowed hard. *Just the facts. Stick to the facts.*

"Doctor Osprey's dead," he said. His voice sounded too flat, too distant, like it belonged to someone else. "He had a seizure of some kind—he was coughing up blood when I got there, and then—" He shuddered helplessly and looked away. "Then he just...*died.*"

Wu stood, shoving back his chair. "Was anyone with him?"

"Zielinski. I—I think Zielinski's in shock." He gulped air, heard his voice go up an octave. "I—I think *I'm* in shock. God, all the blood!"

"Get yourself under control, Colonel."

"Yes, sir." He pressed his eyes shut, stood up straight. Forced a few deep breaths. Struggled to press down the panic.

He opened his eyes and focused on the general. "I'm sorry, sir. It caught me by surprise."

The general motioned toward the hallway. "Let's go."

CHAPTER 15

After the last soldier had been served, Jason helped himself to a tray of food and went out with Yerkins to eat. Cookie had begged off.

"I never eat after service," Cookie said. "I graze as I work, and anyway, I need to start cleanup. Lunch prep begins in two hours. Maybe you'd like to…?" He said it hopefully, as if expecting Jason to volunteer to help with the next meal, but Jason just laughed and shook his head.

"I wish I could, but I have my own work. If I get up early again, though, you can bet I'll stop in and help with breakfast. I had a lot of fun."

As Jason and Yerkins walked out to the tables, a man's deep voice called, "Jase! Over here! I need to talk to you."

It was Clay Washington. He and Terry O'Malley sat at a table with their backs to one of the big windows. They sat by themselves, Jase noted, rather than with the soldiers. Not really part of the team? If it had been him, he would have made a point of eating with the army kids every chance he had.

"Later, Jase," Yerkins said, "I'm going to join my friends. But after those biscuits, I bet they'd like to meet you…?"

"No worries," Jason said. "I'll join you guys for lunch." Turning, he headed for the pair of geologists.

Clay grinned up at him. "You're the news of the day, Jase. These biscuits rock." He took a bite of one as if to emphasize his point.

Chewing slowly, Terry added, "Good eggs, too."

"The eggs and sausage are Cookie's." Jase set his tray down and slid into a chair. "Glad you like the biscuits, though. It's my mother's recipe." He picked up his fork and dug in, and for a few seconds, no one spoke.

Then Clay cleared his throat. "I've been wondering…maybe you'd like to take a walk outside with me?"

"Outside?" Jason looked up from his plate, fork paused midair. "As in, *on the glacier* outside? In the cold?"

"Yeah."

"Is there something worth seeing?"

"I think maybe there is." Clay looked to each side, leaned over conspiratorially, and lowered his voice to a near whisper. "Did you see the huge piles of rock and ice the soldiers have been dumping out there?"

"Sure, from the helicopter." Aside from the base itself, the dumping ground offered the only landscape feature for miles in any direction. "And you can see it from there." He nodded toward the windows behind Clay.

"I don't think you heard it, considering the way you were snoring last night, but the wind came up around one a.m. I couldn't sleep. I lay there and listened to it howl for hours. That's when it hit me."

"What?" Jason said.

"Strong winds scour the glaciers. That's why they're so smooth. Those same winds have also been working on the ice we've been piling up out there for months—it's a big target." He leaned back. "And *that* means, maybe it exposed more of that magic alien metal—or anything else the soldiers missed. It could be sitting out there *right now* just waiting to be picked up. By us."

"Wouldn't it take years to wear down ice?"

"It's not just erosion, it's evaporation. Even in the cold, ice evaporates. We don't need much evaporation to expose anything trapped in the ice."

Jase nodded slowly as he chewed. It sounded possible. But what was the temperature outside now—twenty below? Thirty? *Do I really want to go out there?*

"It's a good idea," he said. More samples might be worth the risk of frostbite. "Is there a process? Do we need to request formal permission? Or sign out?"

Clay shrugged. "I thought we'd just suit up and go. It's not like the door is guarded. No one leaves the building voluntarily, after all."

Jason looked at Terry, who was shaking his head. Clearly he didn't agree.

"What do you think, Terry?" Jason asked. Did he have something else in mind?

"Clay's crazy. It's too damn cold out there. I can barely stand the tunnels. If you want the dump checked, ask Colonel Bloch to send out the soldiers. It's hazard work, and that's their job, not ours. Make them earn their pay."

"We're being well paid, too," Clay pointed out.

"Not that well! I like my fingers and toes, thank you very much."

"Don't be a wuss. We won't be outside long." Clay popped a last piece of biscuit into his mouth and chewed. "Fifteen minutes, maybe half an hour tops. Just long enough to check the exposed surfaces. If we don't find anything, the military never needs to know. Fast in, fast out. What do you say, Jase?"

"I'm in," Jason said. "But I don't want to burn bridges my first day here. We have to tell Bloch and Wu before we go. Sneaking around can only come back and bite us in the ass. What if there are security cameras? Or an alarm on the door? Do you really want to piss them off?"

Clay laughed. "I heard that!"

Terry stared at him. "Heard what?"

"He didn't say *ask* Bloch, he said *tell* him."

"Exactly." Jason smiled. "Never ask when you can tell." That principle had served him well in academia. "Since we're going to be looking for more samples, I can't see him refusing. And if anything happens outside, someone will know where we went."

Terry said, "That's a much better plan."

"Definitely," Clay said. "When do we go?"

"First thing after lunch?" Jason took another bite of eggs. "Is that the warmest part of the day here?"

"I don't think there is a warmest part. But agreed." He looked at Terry. "What do you say, bro? Are you in or out?"

"As long as you're asking Bloch's permission…" Terry sighed, shook his head. "I know I'm going to regret it, but I guess I have to go. Someone needs to keep you two out of trouble."

CHAPTER 16

As they approached the infirmary door, Private Zielinski struggled to snap to attention on his crutches. In less serious circumstances, the general would have found it amusing. Zielinski, dressed in olive-green skivvies, managed a passable salute without falling over, though. Wu returned it.

"Return to the dormitory and get dressed, Private," he said, stopping in front of the man. "Not a word about Doc's death to anyone yet. I will make an announcement about it shortly, when I have more information. Understood?"

"Yes, sir."

"Very good. Dismissed."

"Sir." Zielinski hesitated. "Um, my boots are inside..."

Wu glanced down. The private was barefoot.

"Very well. Colonel, would you assist him?"

"Yes, sir." Bloch ducked into the room and returned a minute later with a pair of boots. They had been cleaned since Zielinski's accident in the tunnel, but the left one showed a few faint blood stains. Bloch passed them to Zielinski, who dropped them to the floor and slipped them on without socks and without bothering to untie them.

"Thank you, sir." The private saluted again, then hobbled down the corridor.

Wu watched him for a second, then turned and motioned Bloch into the infirmary. He noted how the curtain had been pulled back at the middle bed, and he could see Osprey lying there on blood-soaked sheets. A large puddle of blood slowly congealed around and under the bed. Bloch must have stepped in it—bloody footprints led to the door.

He turned to the colonel. "Describe what you saw when you first came into the room."

"The door was closed when I got here," Bloch began, and he told in more detail how he had found the doctor in the midst of a seizure. He swallowed hard and had to pause for a second when he got to the bit about vomiting up blood. "Then—he just died."

Good thing I didn't like the doctor, Wu thought. Osprey hadn't socialized with anyone here, as though he thought himself better than everyone else. Competent, of course—but lacking that friendly bedside manner you wanted from a physician.

Slowly Wu circled the bed, avoiding the blood and peering at Osprey's body from every angle. *Curious.* Under the bright red bloodstains, the man's face had a calm, almost serene expression. *What did I expect, a death rictus?*

"Give me your thoughts," he said.

"I think it might have been a *grand mal* seizure," Bloch said. "I've never seen one, just read about them, so it's only a guess. We'll need an autopsy for sure. The amount of blood was…disturbing. He was vomiting it up by the pint. And I could hear a strange bubbling sound in his chest—like popping bubble wrap, if you know what I mean."

"I've heard it before. It happens when a lung is punctured."

Bloch shuddered. "Maybe something burst inside him?"

"Mm." Did lungs have blood vessels that could burst like that? It seemed unlikely.

Wu looked around the room, spotted a box of tissues, and plucked out three of them. With a few deft twists, he braided them into a wick. From his pocket, he pulled out his father's old silver cigarette lighter. He'd hoped he wouldn't need it, but he'd brought to with him to Antarctica for a reason. Best to make sure, considering the report on the alien he'd read at the Pentagon.

Bloch watched with fascination. "Sir, you don't think the doctor is one of those alien *things*…?"

Fast on the uptake. Wu had to give him points for that.

"Let's just say—I'm keeping an open mind, Colonel." Wu shrugged. "According to the 1939 report, they don't like fire…"

It took two strikes for the lighter to catch a flame, then he set the tissues ablaze and dropped them onto the pool of blood. There, the soft paper flared for a second, fizzled, and went out. A thin, black line of foul-smelling smoke drifted lazily upward.

"Not a monster," Bloch said. He fanned the smoke with his hand to disperse it.

Or the original report was wrong. Wu stared down at the blood.

He'd half expect it to move to avoid the flaming tissues. But of course, no alien creature had leaped into the air or screamed in pain. Nothing had happened, and nothing would.

He let out the breath he found he'd been holding, then gave a derisive snort. *Can't believe I was worried about the doctor being an alien.* Quite ridiculous.

"Occam's razor," Bloch murmured.

"What's that?" Wu glanced over at the colonel.

"Occam's razor—the simplest explanation is usually the best one," Bloch said.

"Occam's razor, yes." He shook his head. *Sometimes a cigar is just a cigar.* "My report will say the doctor had had a fatal seizure. Nothing strange or supernatural about it. And we didn't have the personnel or equipment to save him. Unfortunate, but unavoidable."

"Your fire test—did you really suspect…?"

"Silly of me, I know." Wu forced a laugh, but he couldn't meet the colonel's gaze. "It's easy to become paranoid here." *The confinement, the isolation… God, I need a vacation.*

"And now they have found an alien in the ice."

"Yes." Wu frowned. The timing had to be coincidental. Only he didn't believe much in coincidences.

He said, "Osprey's file didn't mention any pre-existing medical conditions, did it?"

"No, sir. That would have ruled him out for this mission."

"Still, it may have been undiagnosed—or undisclosed. Epilepsy would have kept him out of the army, after all. But only if he admitted it."

"Yes, sir," Bloch said. "And I've heard of epilepsy causing nosebleeds. But never—" He gestured at the body, at the blood. "—*this.* We need an autopsy to figure it out."

No chance of that, Wu thought. It would be cremation for the doctor—and the same for Pieter Oud, and then for the thing in the ice—as soon as that portable crematorium arrived. *Just in case.*

Bloch hesitated. "Or…there is one other possible answer, sir. He's the one person on base with ready access to prescription drugs." He nodded pointedly at the two white medical cabinets. "If he had a bad reaction to something he took…"

"I suppose that's possible, too," Wu said. He frowned. *Occam's razor, again.* But he'd seen the list of medical supplies, and aside from a small quantity of opioids for pain, they had little on hand beyond analgesics and antibiotics. What possible drug combination would cause a fatal seizure?

He continued, "For now, I think it's best to blame a seizure. For morale, if nothing else—everyone understands about seizures. Act of God. No need to disparage Osprey's reputation with even a hint about drug abuse."

"Yes, sir."

Wu turned and regarded the doctor's body. Cookie just about had a fit when he suggested storing Dr. Oud's body in the kitchen's walk-in freezer. How many sanitary regulations would that have violated? They ended up storing Oud's body outside. Osprey's body would have to go out there, too.

"There are body bags in the left-hand cabinet," he said, pointing to one of the white metal cabinets next to the desk. "Get one, and we'll bag him up."

"You mean—us?"

"Afraid of getting your hands dirty, Colonel?" Wu gave him a hard look.

"No, sir. Just caught off guard." He went to the cabinet, tried the handle. "Locked."

"I noticed his keys on the desk," the general said.

"Right, sir." Bloch crossed to the desk and grabbed the small keyring, then fumbled first one, then another into the cabinet's lock. The third key worked. Swinging the door open, he stared at the neatly stacked boxes of supplies.

He's a career bureaucrat, Wu reminded himself. *Never held a field command. Never had to bag-and-tag bodies.* Of course, he wouldn't know what to look for.

Wu said, "Bottom shelf, Colonel—the large white box labelled 'HRP.' That stands for human remains pouch."

Bloch gulped, but pulled out the box and removed a black body bag. Slowly he began to unfold it. A couple of small cards fluttered out and landed on the floor.

"Don't lose those," Wu said.

"What are they?"

"Toe tags."

The body bag was the same size the general remembered—36 inches by 90 inches—but folded up to half the space. *Making them thinner these days*, he thought. It had been a long time since his service in Iraq. Advancements in science touched everything, it seemed.

Bloch laid the bag out on the floor, safely beyond the congealing pool of blood, and together they managed to heave the doctor's body over and into it. Bloch adjusted the sides around the doctor's arms and legs, then started to zip it closed.

Wu stopped him with one hand. "You're forgetting the 'tag' part of 'bag-and-tag'. All bodies need to be identified. We may not be there to say who he is."

Bloch went back to the labels he'd dropped, bent, and picked them up. "Do we need two of them?"

"The first one is for the big toe on his right foot." He stripped off the doctor's shoes—they seemed to be the only part of his clothing not soaked in blood—then his socks. He tucked them in the bag, too. Osprey's flesh was cool, but still supple; rigor mortis had not yet begun to settle in. "The other label goes on the outside of the bag, in that clear plastic sleeve by the head. It's for quick identification."

Silently, Bloch found a pen in the desk drawer and filled out both cards. He handed one to the general, who tied it around the man's toe with its attached string. As he did, Bloch tucked the second label into the clear plastic pouch.

As Wu pulled the zipper up and sealed the doctor's body inside, Bloch seemed to relax for the first time when the man's face vanished behind plastic. *Definitely not used to death,* the general thought.

Now came the hard part—getting the body into the hall.

He bent and grabbed two of the body bag's six handles, and Bloch did the same on the other side. They heaved, got him airborne, and shuffle-walked toward the door with the body between them. Osprey was a lot heavier than he looked. *Or bodies have gotten a lot heavier since my days in Iraq.*

Together, they managed to get the body out into the corridor.

Dead weight, Wu thought and suppressed a laugh.

He found himself breathing hard, and his joints creaked alarmingly. *Not as young as I used to be.* At least his back didn't go out this time. Luckily they had sent Zielinski off before he could see them puffing and sweating. The troops would have laughed about it for a month. Any of them could probably have shifted the body single-handedly.

He and Bloch both gave sighs of relief as they half set, half dropped Osprey's body outside the door. Bloch straightened and pressed his palms hard to his back, but didn't make any complaints.

Wu said, "Lock up the infirmary, then find a couple of men and get them to move the body outside. Put it next to Dr. Oud." Then he realized the doctor had handled Oud's body rather than Bloch. Did the colonel know where they had stored it? He added, "It's in the helicopter landing area, by the far wall."

"Yes, sir. I know where it is."

Of course you do. "Carry on."

He gave a nod, turned, and strolled with forced casualness toward his office. He glanced into the mess hall as he passed, but everyone had cleared out except the two geologists and Jason Cosgrove, who sat by the windows talking over coffee. Cookie was banging pans somewhere in the back, out of sight.

Then he reached the officers' mess, opened the door, and went inside. As expected, their breakfast trays had already been cleared and the tabletop wiped down. But now the table lay completely empty.

Wu froze. *Where the hell are our laptops?*

CHAPTER 17

Nathan Yerkins plugged in his phone and dropped it on top of his pillow. Its battery might be dying a slow and painful death, but it would be fully charged—at least for a couple of hours—when work in the tunnel ended.

He glanced at the clock on the wall: 08:52. Almost time to head down.

Then voices around him called, "Hey, man!" and half a dozen people began to clap and whistle.

He turned toward the door as a grinning Adam Zielinski hobbled in on crutches. Zielinski gave a wave and ducked his head with boyish modesty.

"You feelin' okay, Zee?" Chuck Renner drawled.

"Yeah, yeah." Zielinski maneuvered over to his bed, on the far side of Yerkins. He balanced on one leg while leaning his crutches against the wall, then plopped down on his cot. Everyone clustered around and pounded him on the back.

Like he's some kind of returning hero, Yerkins thought, trying not to roll his eyes, *rather than the goofball who hit himself in the leg with a pickaxe while trying to show off.* That's what you got in this outfit when you had the looks of a young Tom Cruise and the brains of a cocker spaniel. *A smart cocker spaniel, but still...*

Taking a deep breath, Yerkins forced a grin and said, "Welcome back, dude!" along with everyone else.

"*'Ten-SHUN!'*" he heard Seetoo bawl.

Silence fell. Everyone whirled to face front, snapping to attention. General Wu suddenly filled the doorway, looking particularly grim. Yerkins saluted, along with the rest of the men.

Without a word, the general strode forward between the rows of cots, glaring hard at each man as he passed. Someone to his left gulped audibly. Even Zielinski got the full force of the general's stare.

Something's wrong, Yerkins realized. The last time he'd seen an officer this mad had been in basic training, when two recruits had jumped their drill sergeant one night and beaten the crap out of him. The sergeant had been hospitalized. Both men had both been court martialed. *Something's really, really wrong.*

"I have two things to say," the general finally said, voice like a whip.

He didn't tell us "at ease." Yerkins made a silent gulp and held himself rigidly upright. He watched from the corners of his eyes as the general paced, staring hard at each man in turn. *Did he find out I missed my guard shift?*

But the general wasn't focusing just on him—or on anyone in particular.

"First," Wu said, "Dr. Osprey suffered a fatal seizure in the infirmary. There will be a minute of silence for him at dinner tonight. Until we have a replacement medical officer in place, which will take some weeks, I strongly recommend not doing anything stupid to injure yourselves." He paused in front of Zielinski. "Is that understood?"

"Sir! Yes, sir!" everyone said.

"Second," Wu continued, "My laptop and Colonel Bloch's laptop have both been taken from the officer's mess without permission. We left them there while attending to Dr. Osprey. If anyone here moved them, let me know now to avoid future, more unpleasant consequences."

"Sir!" someone at the far end of the room called. Was it Dobbs?

"Yes, Private?" said the general.

"I cleared your table at the end of mess, sir. Your laptops were not there at that time."

Yerkins could have slapped himself—part of his KP duty was not only serving the general, but busing the table afterward—and he'd forgotten. What was wrong with him? He couldn't seem to remember anything anymore.

It's this place, he told himself. *It's breaking me down. It's breaking everyone down.*

But why would someone take the officers' laptops? It wasn't like you could pawn them here. Or do anything with them—there wasn't any privacy, and everyone would know you'd done it. Could it be some kind of prank? But who would dare prank a general...except another general?

"Thank you for that information." Wu's calm tone sounded forced to Yerkins. Then the general addressed the whole room. "Report to your duties. Dismissed."

Yerkins hustled toward the door with the rest of the men. For once, he couldn't wait to get into the tunnel.

CHAPTER 18

Corporal Menendez floored the accelerator and zipped the little golf cart around the row of soldiers straggling down toward the end of the tunnel. Everyone seemed more subdued than usual, despite last night's celebration. She snorted. *Or maybe because of it.* Not all of the army boys could hold their liquor.

She glanced over her shoulder and met more than a few blood-shot gazes. *Definitely because of it.*

Her own head throbbed a bit. She'd swallowed an Advil before breakfast, but it hadn't done more than take the edge off her own hangover. Not that she'd let it show.

She rounded the last switchback, then pulled up next to the mini bulldozer. Kavanaugh perched in the driver's seat, boots up on the console, hands tucked deep in his coat pockets. He stared down at her with his usual hint of a mocking smile.

"You're relieved," she said.

"Thanks, Corporal."

Yawning, he climbed down. "Okay to head up for a shower?" he asked, picking up his breakfast tray. He'd left it balanced on the bulldozer's shovel.

"Sure." She hopped out of the golf cart and looked him over, but he didn't look much worse than usual. "You need some shut-eye?"

"Nah. Give me an hour and I'll be back down to help."

That definitely wasn't like him—not that she'd object. It felt like they were getting near a big discovery down here, and the more hands working, the better.

She gave him a curt nod. "Sure. See you in an hour."

He nodded and started up the ramp. As he passed the other soldiers, she heard him saying something to Chuck Renner, but couldn't hear what. Probably grousing about his guard shift, or the mission in general, or the general's order to stand watch over a frozen whatsit in the ice. He had a whiny-baby streak, as her brother called it. Not as bad as Dobbs, but definitely there.

She looked over the site. The tools and equipment lay where they had been left the day before. The blue tarp, pinned to the wall with pylons, still covered the creature. They'd have to go around, like the general said.

She headed to the end wall where they had been working, drew out her flashlight, and played its beam into the ice to the left. Light caught on fractures, showing a murky two or three feet deep. Nothing big hiding in there that she could see. They could take a ten-foot jog to the side, then turn back and keep going. Easy.

The troops began to gather around her.

"We'll take the tunnel left for twenty feet, then turn back on course," she said. "Platt?"

"Yes, Corporal?" she called from the back.

"You and Renner do the survey. Where's your total station?"

"I brought it down, Corporal." She held up the theodolite with its tripod. The measuring device flashed as an arc light reflected off of its lens. "Knew we'd need it this morning."

"Right. Jump to it. Everyone else, start assembling ceiling braces." She looked up at the ceiling. "We're going to need to reinforce the roof here before we start digging again."

* * * *

General Wu found Bloch waiting outside his office. He opened the door, rounded his desk, and sat heavily. *Intolerable.* They needed those laptops.

Bloch trailed him inside, and Wu waved him into a chair. The colonel settled himself, then leaned forward, hands between his knees, expression earnest and more than a little puzzled.

"Well?" Wu demanded.

"No sign of the laptops. I spoke to everyone in the women's barracks—I'd swear they don't know anything." He shook his head. "And I've already checked my office, the supply room, and Cosgrove's office. Nothing looked out of place."

Wu leaned back. "I think you can eliminate Cosgrove and the civilian geologists as suspects."

"Why, sir?"

"I noticed the three of them talking in the mess hall before and after we went to sick bay. They hadn't moved. No opportunity."

"If we eliminate them," Bloch said slowly, "that just leaves our people. Why would one of them take our laptops?"

"Fatigue?" the general suggested. *Or maybe they're pissed off about being stuck out here and just want to go home.* He cleared his throat. "Security footage?"

"I'll review it next, but I don't think it's going to be much help. We only have cameras in the mess hall and at the entryways. Unless our thief was dumb enough to take the laptops in for breakfast, or carry them into the tunnel—or even outside, for that matter—we won't find them on the recordings."

"Damn it." Wu slapped the desk with the flat of his palm. *Not acceptable.* "There must be something else you can do."

The colonel's gaze grew distant. "It's not like we have MPs to investigate, or a forensics team to fingerprint the crime scene," he pointed out. "The only good news is that we are in a confined space. There aren't that many places for someone to hide a pair of laptops. It's not like you can take them to a pawn shop or sell them on Craigslist from here."

"True." The general drummed his fingertips on the desktop. "A room-by-room search should turn them up…"

Bloch stood. "I'll get right on it. I'll take a couple of men and do a room-by-room search."

"I'll handle the search while you deal with the cameras." Might as well keep busy. Without his laptop, what else could he do? *And if we get another message from Mars, I want to hear it immediately.*

"Yes, sir." Bloch saluted and hurried out.

Wu opened one of his desk drawers and pulled out a small walkie-talkie. He thumbed the power switch and then sent his message:

"Base to Menendez. Come in, please."

A second later, the answer came: "Roger that. Corporal Menendez here, sir. Over."

"Send up three men immediately. Over."

"Yes, sir. Over."

"Base out."

* * * *

Colonel Bloch could have slapped himself. The second he left the general's office, he realized his mistake—he needed his laptop to access the network drive where they stored the security footage from the cameras. Did the base have any other computers he could use? He didn't think any of the soldiers had one—he'd seen a few iPads, but mostly they used phones for everything from email to watching movies. And he couldn't exactly borrow their equipment without permission. That would open a different can of worms.

Then he remembered the metallurgy lab. It had an old computer. And Pieter kept its password stuck to the back of the monitor with a Post-It note. Convenient, if not exactly secure. Besides, who would bother with a Windows 95 machine, anyway?

He hurried down the corridor to the lab. The door was shut. He opened it and went inside, and found the room deserted. No sign of Jason Cosgrove—why wasn't he surprised? If the general hadn't ruled him out, Cosgrove would have been his prime suspect.

Bloch perched on the stool by the computer, hit the space bar, and after a few seconds, the old Windows logo vanished, to be replaced by a modern Linux desktop—the Windows logo had to be a gag screensaver.

He leaned forward and studied the desktop. He'd never seen a more confusing clutter of files. Pieter must not have understood how to use folders.

Shaking his head, he opened a new browser window, typed in the network drive's address. *Might as well start with the outside doors.* He scrolled down to the saved video files and selected the directory labeled Camera Three. A month's worth of saved .mp4 video files sat there, each fifteen minutes long.

How long had they been with Osprey's body? Twenty minutes? Half an hour? Best call it 45 minutes to make sure. Wu would skin him alive if he cut corners and missed something important.

He found the file with the right time-stamp, opened it, and found himself staring at the little airlock leading to the helicopter. No people. No movement.

At high speed, he began to fast-forward through the footage.

CHAPTER 19

Colonel Bloch wasn't in his office or in the general's—the doors to both offices stood open, and Jason could see Wu frowning and writing on a yellow legal pad. He looked absolutely furious. Probably not the best time to bother him.

He peeked into the officers' mess—empty—and opened the doors to various storerooms and a small gym—all empty. The men's barracks only had one man with a bandaged leg lying on his cot, reading an old *Sports Illustrated*.

"Hey," the man said, pushing himself to a sitting position and tossing down the magazine. "You're new?"

"Yeah. I'm Jase Cosgrove, the new metallurgist. I'm looking for Colonel Bloch. Have you seen him?"

"Sorry, not for an hour. Come on in, it's lonely on sick call. Want to play a hand of cards?"

"Sorry, I've got to work. You know."

"Yeah." He shrugged, lay back, picked up the magazine. "I'm Adam Zielinski. Everyone calls me Zee.

"Later, Zee."

Jase ducked out and kept hunting. But Bloch wasn't in any of the other likely places. Had he gone down the tunnel to check on the excavation project? It might be nice to check out the site, but he didn't want to butt in. It had to be a restricted area. If so, the colonel would be back for lunch. Maybe Clay and Terry, who had just gone down themselves, could take the opportunity to ask about the outside trip.

He headed for his office. Might as well dig into Pieter's research and try to get on top of his own job this morning. No sense putting it off. Who knew what tidbits of wisdom he might glean from his old friend's journals.

When he opened his office door, though, he found Colonel Bloch perched on a stool using his laptop. He blinked. Bloch paused a video he had been scanning.

"I was just looking for you," Jason said, "but I never thought to look in here."

"I wouldn't be here if someone hadn't made off with General Wu's and my laptops," Bloch grumbled. "I needed to borrow yours to review security footage. I'm afraid this has to take priority for now."

"At least the culprits can't get far."

Bloch gave him a withering look.

"Uh, anyway, sure—I was planning to read Pieter's journals today and take notes, so I don't need the laptop. You're welcome to it. Why don't you take it to your office?"

"Good. Thanks." He reached down and yanked the power cable.

"Anyway, I wanted to talk to you because Clay had what sounded like a great idea to me. He wants to go outside to the ice dump and look over everything that's been hauled out of the tunnel." Quickly he explained Clay's theory about the wind speeding evaporation and exposing more pieces of the alien metal.

Bloch nodded thoughtfully as he tucked the laptop under his arm. "Yes, more samples are a priority. When did you want to go?"

"After lunch today."

"I'll check with General Wu, but I see no problem. I'll send a couple of people out with you. You should limit exposure—no longer than twenty minutes outside. Don't get lulled in by a false sense of security. This continent's a killer. Never forget that."

"Noted."

As Bloch hurried up the corridor toward his office, Jason settled himself on the stool, then began pulling Pieter's papers and notebooks out of the satchel and sorting them by date. There had to be thousands of pages.

He groaned and picked up the first one. Best to start at the beginning.

* * * *

By the time they reached the end of the excavation tunnel, Clay and Terry were out of breath and huffing. Clay hadn't realized how late it had gotten. They had hustled all the way down to join the rest of the team.

Corporal Menendez looked up from her iPad and frowned. "You're late," she said. "Work begins at 09:00 sharp. We've been down here for nearly 20 minutes already. If you weren't civilians, you'd be on report."

"I'm so sorry," Terry said. Clay glanced over at him, and he had his sad-puppy look going. "We were talking to Jase about a new project and lost track of time."

"New project?" she asked. Her eyebrows raised. "Anything that affects us down here?"

"Maybe," Clay said. "It's going to depend on Bloch and Wu."

He explained, and she gave a curt nod. She got it. Most of the soldiers here wouldn't see the big picture if you hung it six inches in front of their eyes. But he'd always had a feeling she knew more than she let on, but dumbed things down to fit in with the jocks and jarheads.

"Just be on time in the future," she said. "When you're late, it sets a bad example."

"Won't happen again," Terry said.

"Yeah," Clay said. "So, what do you want us to do today? More wall smoothing?"

She thrust her chin toward the men shifting a stack of steel girders. "Lieutenant Peck mapped out the detour around the, ah, *sea lion*—" Clay gave a derisive snort, and she turned a glare on him. "—last night. We have to add more ceiling braces because we've created a larger chamber than she originally specced. Help Dobbs and Hammond shift the girders, then I'll find you something else."

Girders—great. Clay gave a mental sigh, but didn't let Menendez see. They'd have to dig out the muscle ointment tonight. Strange, how they always got the hardest work duties when they managed to piss her off.

* * * *

"General, I don't suppose the laptops turned up—or anyone stopped by to turn them in?" Colonel Bloch asked from the doorway.

"Nothing. Any luck with the camera feeds?"

He shook his head. "No suspicious activity at all."

Wu frowned, stared at the ceiling. "I would swear none of the men knew anything about the laptops. I took a good, long look at them when I told them about the theft, and none showed the slightest guilty reaction." He leaned back in his chair. "Surprise, yes, and a bit of concern. But nothing more than that. And Yerkins has screwed something up again, but not this. Might want to look into that when you have time."

Yerkins… The colonel shook his head. He'd completely fallen apart over the last two months. He pulled a small notepad and stub of a pencil from his breast pocket and made a note. Probably not worth his attention, especially now when had to focus on the missing laptops.

He said, "If you rule out the men's dorm, that's three-fourths of the people here. But the rest—" He shook his head. "Cookie doesn't know how to use a computer, Osprey's dead, and I know the women's psych profiles. This theft doesn't fit anyone here. I'd say the geologists or Cosgrove would be the most likely candidates, if you hadn't already ruled them out."

"Did you learn anything at all when you reviewed the videos?"

"Only by process of elimination. I know where the laptops aren't—and they definitely aren't outside."

"Which means they're somewhere in here with us." Wu's fingers drummed on the desktop for a second. "That gives us a place to start. Get a couple of men up here, and we'll begin the search."

"Do you have anyone in mind, sir? Or do you want me to pick them?"

"Yes. Use those two geologists. And Cosgrove."

Bloch met the general's gaze. "It might be better to keep this an internal matter. They are civilians"

"They're part of the team, like it or not, Colonel. Unless you can think of any better candidates? Anyone we know definitively didn't take them—other than you, me, and Zielinski?"

"Very good, sir. I'll get them started. In the meantime…" He ducked away to his own office, snagged Cosgrove's laptop, and brought it back to the general. "Cosgrove loaned me his computer to review the video files. You might want to conscript it, until yours reappears."

The general held out his hands, face breaking into a cold smile. "Best news of the morning." *I need to see if there are any new Mars reports.*

CHAPTER 20

Clay heard static and a muffled voice from Menendez's walkie-talkie, but couldn't make out more than a word or two—had someone just said "geologists"? He paused to watch as she deliberately strolled away from the work area.

"Come on, grab your end," Terry said. He was bent over one of the steel beams, knees bent, ready to lift.

"Hold up," Clay said. He took a step toward Menendez, staring. "I think we may have a reprieve coming."

"You sure?" Terry stood, rubbing his back.

Clay nodded toward the corporal. "I'm pretty sure I heard someone mention us over the walkie-talkie. Might have been Bloch"

"Why?"

"Dunno."

Menendez raised the walkie-talkie, spoke into it, listened, spoke again. This time Clay couldn't make out any of the words. But she turned and shot him and Terry a glance, frowned, then beckoned them over.

Clay led the way. "What's up?" he asked her.

"The colonel wants to see you ASAP. Report to his office."

He exchanged a glance with Terry. "Did he say why?"

"The colonel doesn't tell me anything, except what to do. Maybe he's going to dress you down for not pulling your weight. It takes you twice as long to do the same work as Dobbs and Hammond."

"They're a lot younger and fitter than us—" Terry began.

"She's yanking your chain," Clay said. He gave Terry a light punch on the arm. "Lighten up, man. Have a sense of humor."

"Yeah, don't get all defensive," Menendez said. She gave a wicked grin. "If I had to guess, I say it's about your outside trip."

"Oh," Terry said. His cheeks grew flushed.

"Aw, you're cute when you're embarrassed."

Terry looked away, face reddening further.

"Leave him alone," Clay said. "He does his best." He turned to

Terry. "Jase must have talked to Bloch about it."

"Makes sense," Terry muttered.

Clay said, "Thanks for the good news, Menendez. See you at lunch. Come on, Terry." He started up the tunnel.

"I'll save you a few girders," Menendez called after them.

"Don't let her get under your skin," Clay said, as soon as they rounded the corner.

* * * *

It took less than ten minutes to make it to Bloch's office. Clay rapped on the door frame, but the colonel had already seen them. Grim-faced, he stood and moved out from behind his desk.

"Did Jase talk to you about our outside project?" Clay asked.

"Yes, but that's not what this is about. Follow me."

Turning, they headed up the corridor toward the general's office.

Clay exchanged a puzzled glance with Terry. If this wasn't about the trip outside, what was it about? Why the game of hiding the reason? Bloch might not like or trust them, but he'd always been fair and straightforward before.

Bloch passed the general's office and led the way to Jason's lab. The door stood open. Inside, Jason sat hunched over his worktable, with two of Pieter's composition books open in front of him. He scribbled furiously on a yellow legal tablet.

"Dr. Cosgrove," Bloch said.

Jase jumped a bit as though startled, straightened and turned. He looked at the three of them, then seemed to shake himself back to the here and now. *That's focus,* Clay thought.

"Sorry to interrupt," Bloch said. "But the general has a new project for the four of us."

Jason cocked his head, lips tightening. "The laptops?" he asked.

"Yes." Bloch turned to Clay and Terry. "The general saw you three sitting in the mess hall when we went to sick bay to see Dr. Osprey, and you hadn't moved on his way back to the officers' mess. He ruled you three out as suspects because of this. I spent the last couple of hours going through security footage on Jason's computer, and nobody left the compound. So we know the laptops are still on the base...somewhere."

"And we get to find them," Clay said. That made sense. And it

THE THINGS FROM ANOTHER WORLD | 105

certainly beat hauling steel girders up and down tunnels.

"Exactly," Bloch said. "We are going to split into two search teams. You and Dr. Cosgrove are one. O'Malley and I are the other."

"Wouldn't the soldiers be better suited for this?" Terry asked uneasily.

"You want the person who took them to search for them?" Bloch demanded.

Terry gulped. "I…guess that doesn't make sense."

"Damn straight."

"Where do we start?" Clay asked.

"Here." Bloch gestured around Jason's lab. "Poke into every box and cubby capable of holding a pair of laptops. Once we're done, we split up and go different directions. Since all three buildings are connected, we will meet up on the other side. There are only so many places the laptops could be stashed. You can skip the general's and my quarters. They are locked when we aren't inside, but everywhere else is fair game. Sing out if you find anything."

"What about the barracks?" Terry said. "I wouldn't want to violate anyone's privacy—"

"Open every trunk and toss every mattress. This is the army. There's no such thing as privacy."

"Okay," he said doubtfully.

"We need those laptops in order to function," Bloch said. "This is not a joke. Or if it's a joke, it isn't a funny one."

CHAPTER 21

Jason helped search his own office, even though he knew it was pointless. He'd gone through the room earlier that morning looking for legal tablets, after all. *But if I object, it might look like I'm trying to cover something up,* he thought. The last thing he needed was an adversarial relationship with Bloch.

Dutifully, though, he poked around behind stacks of papers and the microscope, just in case. You couldn't have hidden anything larger than a postcard in this room, except in the two-drawer filing cabinet. That's where he'd found the legal tablets—along with stacks of the composition books Pieter had favored

"Aha!" Clay cried.

"What?" Bloch turned swiftly.

The geologist held up an amber-colored bottle with a stack of red plastic cups turned upside down over its neck.

"Pietr was holding out on us. He had a secret stash of Jameson behind the filing cabinet."

Jason nodded to himself. That was Pietr's brand, all right. Why hadn't he thought to look back there? Pietr *always* had a bottle stashed somewhere.

"Anything else hidden?" Bloch asked.

Clay set the bottle down and leaned forward, peered over the cabinet again. "A box of pens. Blue ballpoints"

Colonel Bloch snorted.

"Clearly the laptops aren't here," Jason said. Time to move on.

Terry asked, "How many more rooms to go?"

"Too many," Bloch said grimly. He led the way out into the corridor. "Come on, this could easily take all day."

Jase trailed everyone out, shutting the door behind him. All day? He gave a mental sigh. Finding the laptops might be important to Bloch and the general, but he had better things to do with his time. Why didn't they have the soldiers searching instead of him?

"Cosgrove, you and O'Reilly start with the radio room to the right," Bloch said. "Washington and I will go left to the storeroom." He strode briskly to the next door. A handwritten sign taped next to it said, "Storeroom #1,"

"Got it," Jason said to Bloch's back. He glanced at Terry, who shrugged.

For some reason, the next door on their side didn't have any of the hand-written signs that seemed to be all over the base. If the colonel hadn't called it the radio room, he would have assumed it was a closet or maybe an executive washroom.

The door was unlocked, and when he pulled it open, he found a tiny, dark room. Barely more than a closet. He reached inside, felt around until he found the light switch, and flipped it on. Fluorescent tubes flickered to life overhead.

Not much to see. He glanced over a rolling office chair, a table holding some kind of fancy radio apparatus, and a waist-high storage cabinet the same shade of olive green as the one in his own office. A bulky set of headphones sat on the seat of the chair, trailing a wire to the radio.

Behind him, Terry said, "Why would anyone want to take their laptops?"

Jason shrugged. How should he know?

"Seriously, it doesn't make sense," Terry said. "There's no upside to it. You can't sell them, you can't use them, and when you're caught—which you will be, since there's no way to hide anything here for long—you're going to be punished."

"Maybe Wu and Bloch pissed someone off?"

"Well, Dobbs wasn't happy about pulling guard duty last night… but that was Corporal Menendez's decision."

"We'll probably find out when we locate the laptops."

The supply cabinet was the obvious place to look—it was certainly big enough to hold a couple of computers. Jason pulled open the double-doors and glanced over the shelves. It held stacks of what looked like log books, a couple of boxes of pens, a coil of coaxial cable, and some network cables. Probably for the radio antenna. He peeked behind the cabinet just to make sure the laptops weren't there. Nothing—no bottles of whiskey, no pens, not even a dust bunny.

"Uh…Jase?"

He turned. Terry held up a power cable, his face grim. One end connected to the radio apparatus. Instead of a plug, the other end had been chewed to shreds. No way could that power anything, let alone the radio.

Jason felt a chill sweep through him. *This* was no prank.

Terry said, "What do you think? A pack of mice? A giant rat?"

"Looks more like a polar bear did it."

Terry snorted. "Yeah, I often see polar bears roaming the base, looking for wires to chew. Someone doesn't want us talking to the outside world, Jase. This was *deliberate*."

"I better tell Bloch," Jason said. "Wait here."

He jogged over to Storeroom #1 and paused in the doorway to look it over. Rows of steel shelving units full of brown and white cardboard boxes lined the walls. Some boxes had cryptic numbers stenciled on their sides. Others said simply "Mouthwash," "Shaving Lotion," "Tampons," and other essentials. *Figures the army would use generic products.* On top of the shelves sat industrial-sized packages of toilet paper, paper towels, and tissue boxes, all neatly shrink wrapped. *Everything you need to keep a base this size running independently for months,* Jason thought.

"Colonel," Jason said, "you need to see something."

"The laptops?" Bloch glanced up from an open box labeled "Razors (Male)—2,500 Count."

"No." Jason lowered his voice. "Sabotage in the radio room."

"No way!" said Clay.

Bloch sucked in a sharp, angry breath, shoved the box of razors back onto a shelf, and turned to face Clay. "Keep looking, Washington," he said in a calm voice. Then he turned and motioned for Jason to precede him to the radio room. "Let's take a look."

Jason led the way in silence. The damaged power cable would speak for itself. And it had to be sabotage—there couldn't possibly be rats here in Antarctica, and targeting the radio equipment struck him as singularly suspicious. He'd seen enough spy movies to know you took out the enemy's communications first.

But why chew up the wire that way? Anyone with a basic knowledge of electricity could fix it in a few minutes. Why not simply cut it with a knife? It didn't make sense. Or were they *supposed* to believe rats had done it?

He paused at the radio room and let Bloch enter first. Terry now sat in the office chair, holding the end of the power cord. Mutely, he held it up for inspection.

Bloch took it, examined it closely for a few seconds, then let it drop. His frown deepened.

Then he turned and took a clipboard from a hook on the wall by the door. What was that? Jason hadn't noticed it when they came inside. He inched forward until he read it over the colonel's shoulder. It had names, dates, times, and signatures. Some kind of duty roster?

"Join Washington in the storeroom and keep searching for the laptops," Bloch said to them. "I'll inform General Wu. And…" He hesitated. "Keep an eye out for any other damage. Clearly, we have a larger problem than originally thought."

CHAPTER 22

"That's lunch!" Corporal Menendez called, watching the clock on her iPad tick over to 12:30.

Around her, everyone began setting down tools. The mini bulldozer's dull rumble grew still. Laughing and joking, everyone started on the leisurely stroll up toward the surface and food. An hour for lunch, then they'd be back down here till five-thirty.

She lingered in the driver's seat of the golf cart, checking off the last few items in Lieutenant Peck's revised tunnel blueprints on her iPad. The girders looked to be in the right positions. They had done a good job following Peck's plans.

Menendez turned on the iPad's camera and snapped pictures to document everything for Bloch and the general. *It doesn't count unless you can prove it's done and done right.* She hit UPLOAD and watched the transfer-bar zip across. Gotta give the techies credit, they had the wifi working better here than at home, even down in the tunnel.

"Corporal," a voice said behind her.

She turned. It was Yerkins, and he had a funny look on his face.

"Why are you still here, Yerk?" she asked. "Aren't you hungry?"

Silently, he held something out to her—an iPhone, she saw as she took it. The screen was badly cracked, and dark reddish-brown splotches covered it. It looked like…blood splatter? She frowned. *Not good. Definitely not good.*

"It was jammed against one of the 'dozer's wheels," Yerkins said, waving at the front left tire. "You couldn't see it when you're standing. But when I bent down to tie my boot, I spotted it."

She turned the phone over. No name on the back. She doubletapped the screen, but it didn't come to life. Either the battery had died or whatever had cracked the screen had killed it. Most likely the battery, though.

"Do you know who it belongs to?" she asked.

He shrugged. "No idea. But is it covered in *blood*?"

"Yeah. Weird."

Even weirder than a soldier losing his phone.

She scratched at one of the blood spots with her fingernail. It flaked off. Completely dry. It hadn't happened recently—not on this shift, anyway. Not that she could have missed it if someone got injured badly enough to bleed out like this.

Always pass the problem up the chain of command. That was the army way. Eventually someone would handle it.

She bit her lip, then gestured to the seat beside her. "Hop aboard. I'm heading upside now. I'll give the phone to the colonel. Whatever it is, it's above our pay grade."

Yerkins nodded and walked around to the passenger seat. After he climbed in, she floored the accelerator.

At a stately 12 miles per hour, they headed for the surface.

CHAPTER 23

Bloch had expected an explosion of anger from the general when he made his report, but what he got was far worse—silence, a distant look, a blanched, sick expression. One minute stretched to two, then three. Was he all right?

"Sir?" Bloch said at last. He shifted uneasily.

"Let me see the duty log."

Bloch handed over the clipboard from the radio room. General Wu ran his finger down the list of names. "Petersen," he said quietly, "signed in last. Two A.M. Her relief didn't sign in. That would be…" He frowned. "Jooles?"

"Yes, sir." Very sloppy. "Clearly we need to review procedures with the radio team."

"I fear," the general said slowly, setting down the clipboard, "I have made a terrible mistake." Then he reached out and closed Jason's laptop. The computer fan whirred for a few more seconds more, then shut off. Silence stretched between them. The general's gaze remained distant, distracted. What did he know that he wasn't letting on?

"Whoever did it, we'll find them," Bloch finally said. "And I'll have Petersen and Jooles on report."

"At this point, I'm concerned about the big picture." Wu glanced up at him. "Remember the original report, Colonel."

"Sir?" Bloch frowned. What did he mean?

But the general's attention suddenly flicked to the doorway. He raised one hand and motioned someone forward.

"Come in, Corporal. What is it?"

"Sorry to bother you, sirs," Corporal Menendez said, looking between the two of them, "but Private Yerkins found this in the tunnel and turned it in."

She held out a cell phone. Bloch took it, turned it over. Cracks and—was that blood? He raised his eyebrows.

"—why not ask around and see who owns it?" the general was

saying.

Bloch said, "Because it's covered in blood, sir." He set it down on the desk in front of the general. Wu looked down at it, then gave a half nod as if it confirmed something he already suspected.

"You did right, Corporal," Wu said. "We will handle it from here." He paused then added almost as an afterthought, "I haven't had a chance to read your report yet—who was on guard duty last night?"

"First Dobbs, then Seetoo, Renner, Yerkins, and Kavanaugh," she said without hesitation. "Three-hour shifts."

He nodded. "Go get lunch. Dismissed."

"Thank you, sir." She saluted, then turned and withdrew.

As soon as she was gone, the general picked up the phone and tried to power it on. No luck; it was dead. He opened his desk drawer, pulled out a spare iPhone charging cable, and plugged it in.

"Yerkins…" Bloch mused aloud. "Strange, how his name keeps turning up. This morning, you said you thought he was hiding something. Then he pulled guard duty last night. Now he's turned in a bloody iPhone."

"I don't think he's our thief." The general tapped the desk twice with his index finger decisively. "Before we do anything, let's see if we can find out who this phone belongs to. Yerkins wouldn't have turned it in if he owned it—or if he knew to whom it belonged. We have plenty of time to interview him, if necessary."

"Yes, sir." That made sense.

The iPhone's screen suddenly flashed and came to life. Bloch focused on it. One percent power.

"Aha! As I suspected, just needs a little juice." The general pulled the phone closer. He gestured vaguely toward the door. "Close it and have a seat."

Bloch did as instructed, then leaned forward to watch. In a minute, the phone ticked over to two percent power. When it hit three percent, the general pressed the power button, and the login screen popped up. The number pad was clearly visible beneath the spider-web of cracks and the spatters of dried blood.

"Of course, there's a password," Bloch said.

"Always start with the obvious," the general said. "This is the army. We aren't dealing with geniuses."

With a blunt forefinger, he tapped 1-1-1-1-1-1 and got an error message. Next, he tried 1-2-3-4-5-6. This time the home screen opened.

Bloch gave a snort. "Best and brightest be damned," he muttered. These days, you'd think soldiers would know better than to use a password like that.

Wu smiled and tapped a few more buttons. "Intelligence released a report on the most common passwords a few years back. Interesting reading. You should hunt it down when we get home." He tapped the screen a few more times. When he got to the registration screen, he read aloud: "Timothy Seetoo."

"Seetoo!" Bloch said. He met the general's gaze. "He's never without his phone. And he was on guard duty last night."

"That fits," the general said. He turned back to the iPhone and began to thumb through Seetoo's installed programs. "There are some unusual apps here. Why would he have voice dictation software? Microsoft Office? Adobe Photoshop? There doesn't seem to be a single game. What is he, some kind of reporter—or a spy?"

"He fancies himself a writer," Bloch said. He thought back to Seetoo's file. "All fiction, though. According to our records, he published a few stories in magazines. Nothing literary, just sci-fi adventure crap. Juvenile stuff, nothing to do with the military."

"Huh. If that's the case, let's see what he's been working on." The general opened a few programs, thumbed through them, then finally announced, "This seems to be his most recent file—it's dated last night. An audio file."

"I bet he dictates his work while on guard duty," Bloch said. Better than playing the latest Angry Birds or Candy Crush games, as quite a few other soldiers did.

Wu tapped the playback icon, and Private Seetoo's voice emerged from the phone's tiny speaker: *"Chapter Nine. In the tunnel."*

Before Seetoo could say another word, though, there came a surprised yelp, a crashing sound like the phone had been dropped, and rough panting.

"What the hell?" Seetoo's voice continued after a minute. *"How did you get back here—I just saw you leave!"*

Another voice said: *"That—wasn't—me."*

Bloch frowned. He knew that voice. Dobbs?

More panting. A gasp. A strange, horrible gurgling noise.

Desperately, Seetoo's voice cried out: *"Let—me—go!"*

A chill went through Bloch. He glanced at his superior, but the general had his head cocked to one side, a hundred percent focused on the phone.

Gasping, choking sounds. A pained gasp.

Then Seetoo's voice rose again, almost a scream: *"No!"*

A strange, terrible, wet burbling followed, then a final, pathetic whimper. After that, the recording played back silence. It stretched on and on.

After two or three minutes of nothing, the general tapped the STOP button and looked up at him.

Bloch swallowed hard. "What the hell?"

"I think," the general said softly, "we just heard Private Seetoo's death."

Bloch stared. "Impossible. I saw him in the mess hall this morning—"

"I think…I think that wasn't Seetoo. Or, perhaps I should say, not *our* Seetoo." He swallowed hard and looked away. "I think—I think the thing from the tunnel has escaped."

The colonel thought back to the Army file on the 1938 flying saucer incident. Its fantastic story of a shape-shifting alien secretly taking over the bodies of men at a research base had seemed crazy. But was it crazier than everything that had happened since they'd reached Antarctica? Was it crazier than tunneling down to a spaceship buried here for millions of years? Or finding a million-year-old monster trapped in the ice?

"So you think there are two Seetoos running around?" he said.

"Maybe. Or one imitation Seetoo and one—something else."

"I don't follow you, sir. Something else?"

The general leaned back in his chair and steepled his fingers. "Assume for a minute that the original 1938 report is a hundred percent true and accurate to the last detail. They found an alien that could imitate people perfectly once it absorbed their bodies. It even had complete access to their memories."

"That's crazy—" Bloch began. He'd thought the original 1938 largely make-believe, with just a core of truth—the existence of a spaceship.

The general waved him to silence. "Let me finish, Colonel. Can you make that assumption?"

"Yes, sir." He sighed, but nodded.

"Very well. Then let us further assume that we have found another, nearly identical alien. It has the same ability to absorb and imitate people. And it does its work so perfectly that it can walk among us undetected."

"Is that what you think, sir?" Bloch asked. "That one of us is an alien? Do you know how insane that sounds—?"

Wu held up his hand. Bloch shut up.

"This is my proposed sequence of events, Colonel," Wu went on. "First, Private Dobbs is assigned to guard duty. After everyone else leaves the tunnel, he settles down for his shift. But somehow, the alien frees itself from the ice, attacks him, and absorbs his body, including his memories. It fools Seetoo when he shows up. That's what we heard on the recording. Do you follow me so far?"

"Yes, sir."

"Now, because the alien absorbed Dobbs, it has an extra hundred and sixty pounds of mass to deal with, which is a problem. Everyone would notice immediately if Dobbs doubled in weight overnight. And his uniform would no longer fit. So the alien divides in two—maybe it reproduces by fission, like an amoeba, but on a larger scale."

"So now we have two of Dobbs?" Bloch said. "Both aliens?"

"Exactly. Or one Dobbs and one—something else. I'm sure these things have their own original form. But for our purpose, based on this recording, we will say it's a second Dobbs, identical to the first. When Seetoo shows up, he relieves the first imitation of Dobbs, which is wearing Dobb's uniform and passes for human. It returns to base. The second imitation hides. It can't go back to base because it doesn't have a uniform, and a naked Dobbs wandering the halls would attract unwanted attention."

"So the second imitation Dobbs is here to attack and absorb Seetoo once his guard is down?"

"Exactly." Wu leaned back. "Seetoo thought he'd have a quiet night, so he began to dictate more of his book. That's what we heard on the phone. He had just started a new chapter when the second imitation came out, took him by surprise, and absorbed him. He dropped his phone in the process."

"So now we have two imitation Seetoos and one imitation Dobbs."

"And they—or it, if it's one organism in many parts—could repeat the process all night. We effectively set up a conveyor belt to deliver fresh soldiers to it—to them—every three hours."

Bloch said, "Renner relieved Seetoo, then Yerkins relieved Renner—" He broke off. "But that doesn't make sense, sir."

"In what way?" Wu demanded.

"If the alien absorbed Yerkins, why would it turn in Seetoo's iPhone? He'd have access to Seetoo's memories. He'd have known to whom it belonged and how it got there."

"Good point." The general leaned forward, fingers drumming on the desktop. Bloch could see him working through the question. "Maybe there's a limit to how many people this thing can absorb in one day. Perhaps Dobbs and Seetoo were it. Maybe Renner, too. But it couldn't absorb Yerkins, so it had to let him go. He's not much of a threat, after all."

"Perhaps Occam's razor applies," Bloch said.

"You have a simpler explanation?"

"Several occur to me. First, Yerkins has been screwing up a lot lately. You know that—he's been on report four times in the last month. Minor, stupid stuff. This place has affected his work. What if he slept through his guard shift and never showed up to relieve Private Renner?"

Wu slapped the desktop. "Yes! That explains his guilty reaction this morning. Imitation-Renner and imitation-Kavanaugh wouldn't report him because they wouldn't want to attract attention to last night's events." He gave a bark of a laugh. "And that means Renner and Kavanaugh have been absorbed. So there must be at least five of these things loose on base."

"If we follow that line of logic," Bloch said, frowning, "they would try to pick us off one by one, as they find us alone. A radio operator alone in the radio room last night would be a good target…"

"Or someone alone in the infirmary…"

Block sucked in a breath. "The doctor—"

"I was thinking of Zielinski," the general said. "But what if he waited for the doctor, tried to absorb him, but somehow botched it? Maybe the doctor's epilepsy threw him."

Bloch found himself nodding. "Yes. Could be. Or maybe the doctor was playing dead."

"No." Wu shook his head. "Their operation requires secrecy, especially at first. They must move silently among us, catching us when we are alone and off guard. That means sticking to the base's routine. What could be gained by Lieutenant Osprey pretending to be dead?"

"Not a lot, I guess."

General Wu opened his desk drawer and pulled out a sheet of paper. Bloch recognized it as a copy of their staff list. Using a pen, the general began making notes next to names:

PFC Dobbs — yes
PFC Seetoo — yes
PFC Renner — yes
PFC Kavanaugh — yes

After a second, he added:

PFC Zielinski— ? probable
Specialist Petersen —? probable
Specialist Jooles — ? probable

He drew a line through Lieutenant Osprey's name.

"Am I missing anyone who would have been alone at any point last night?" he asked.

"I don't think so, sir."

The general tapped Dobbs's name with the tip of his pen.

"Dobbs," he said. His eyes widened. "He was here earlier, asking for a word with me in private. Then you showed up, and he took off. I think…" He grimaced, looked away. "I think maybe I had a lucky escape." He focused on Bloch again. "You said several explanations presented themselves. Give me another one."

"With all due respect, sir…what if it's *us*? What if we're the ones suffering from paranoid delusions? Some sort of shared psychosis? Aliens taking over human bodies and duplicating people down to their memories, spaceships from Mars—you have to admit it's pretty far out there."

The general gave him a brittle smile. "You're calling bullshit."

"Sir—"

Wu waved him to silence. "I don't blame you. I know it's unbelievable. All of it. I know I'm sleep deprived, and I know I'm not operating at full capacity. Maybe I *am* paranoid—but that doesn't mean they aren't out to get us. I have nightmares every night I'm here, and more than once, I've come awake screaming. I'd like nothing more to be wrong. To find out I *am* crazy. But I don't think I am. Nor are you. Just because we're paranoid doesn't mean this alien—these *things*—aren't out to get us."

"I'm just presenting possibilities, sir."

"Be straight with me. What *do* you believe?"

Bloch met his gaze. "I…have an open mind. I haven't seen much evidence of aliens. I just have your word about the thing in the ice; I haven't been down there to see it myself. But the sabotage in the radio room, on top of Seetoo's recording, on top of the stolen laptops… Taken together, they make a compelling argument that something is very wrong here. I just—I just don't understand *what*. And I'm not ready to accept that it's an alien invasion."

Wu took a deep breath and seemed to draw on some inner reserve of strength. "We need to get ahead of the curve. There has to be something we can do." He stood decisively. Bloch watched him put Jason's laptop and Seetoo's phone into a drawer in his desk, then lock the drawer with a key from the ring in his pocket. Clearly he wasn't going to let them disappear the way their laptops had.

"What do you suggest, sir?" Bloch asked cautiously. ""Do you have a plan?"

"It's lunch time. No one will be back at the work site for at least another half hour. Let's you and me take a ride down the tunnel. If the alien in the ice is gone, we'll know for sure it's loose. And if it's not, we'll look for another explanation."

Bloch thought about it for a heartbeat, then inclined his head. A fair plan. They needed proof to settle things once and for all. *Even if it is aliens.*

CHAPTER 24

Yerkins had waited for her outside the general's office, and he joined her on the walk to the mess hall. She went through the door first—and stopped abruptly just inside. Something inside her said, *There's something wrong.*

Yerkins bumped into her from behind, muttered an apology, and stepped around beside her. He also paused.

She couldn't put her finger on it, but something was off in the room. *Nobody's eating or talking*, she suddenly realized. A dozen soldiers sat silently at a single long table, trays in front of them. No joking. No horseplay. Their food looked like it hadn't been touched, either.

And where were the others? There should have been twice as many people here. Nobody missed lunch.

Then, as if on cue, everyone at the table turned to look at her. Renner, Dobbs, Kavanaugh, Seetoo, Zielinski, Jooles, all the rest—they had bland, neutral expressions, like children trying to look innocent when caught with fingers in a cookie jar.

Hungry— a voice whispered in the back of her head.

"Not too creepy," Yerkins muttered. "You think they practiced that move?"

"Synchronized head spin?" she whispered back. "Yeah. I think they'd have to, to get it so perfect."

And then an unpleasant thought came to mind: *Why do I feel like I've walked in on something nasty?*

"What's up, guys?" she called.

When she met Chuck Renner's gaze, a coldness swept through her. She shuddered and had to look away. Why did his eyes feel so *dead*?

Renner rose and faced her. "Hey, Corporal," he drawled, sounding just like his normal self. "Hey, Yerk. What kept you. We've been waitin'."

Menendez said cautiously, "What's up? Having a meeting of

some kind?"

"Naw, just digestin' our meals." He grinned and patted his belly. Never mind that he hadn't touched the food on his tray. "You're in for a treat today. Remember breakfast? Well, Cookie's on a roll. He made a batch of chicken gumbo. It ain't *Texas* gumbo, but it's real good. He's got it simmerin' on the stove. Come on back and I'll serve you up a batch." He took a few steps toward the kitchen, then paused and half turned. "You hungry, or what?"

So hungry— the voice whispered in the back of her head. *So hungry*—

"Where's Cookie?" she asked. She couldn't see him anywhere. He usually manned the counter at lunch time. The "personal touch" he called it.

"In the storeroom."

"Cookie's taking inventory," said Zielinski. He also stood. "I want another biscuit while there's still some left."

"Cookie made biscuits, too?" Yerkins said. He was all but drooling, Menendez thought. "He never makes biscuits!"

Hungry, that faint voice whispered. *So hungry*—

"Special batch." Renner grinned. "Just like Jason's. Maybe even better. I think Cookie was feelin' inspired."

She felt her stomach rumble. It *had* been a long time since breakfast.

"Cookie needs to order more spices," Dobbs added, standing, "for flavor. That's why he's in the storeroom." He smiled. "I think I'll have seconds, too. While there's still some left. Those biscuits are amazing."

Suddenly, everyone began muttering about biscuits and second helpings and rising.

So hungry— the voice in her head whispered. *So hungry*—

"Line up back of Corporal Menendez and Yerk," Renner said to the others. "They go first, since they ain't had nothin' yet." He turned to face her. "Y'all got here just in time. There ain't many biscuits left."

So hungry—

"I'm down for that!" Yerk crossed to the serving counter and grabbed a tray, but Menendez took a step backwards. She had a weird feeling inside. Nothing she could put a finger on, exactly, but every fiber of her body screamed, *"Run!"*

Kavanaugh smiled at her. "You coming, Corporal?"

Hungry, that soft voice whispered. *So hungry—*

"I don't think so," she said. She could feel her heart pounding. The room seemed to sway a little. "I'm...not feeling well. Maybe the tunnel got to me. I think—I think I better go lie down."

"I can walk you to the infirmary, if you want," Seetoo said. He stepped around the table and headed toward her. "I know where Dr. Osprey keeps his aspirin. That might help."

Hungry—

"Yeah," said Yerkins. "You don't look too good, Corporal. Maybe you should take something."

"I— I'll be fine. I just— I think I need—some air—"

So hungry—

Turning, she stumbled out into the hallway. Hand against the wall for balance, she fled back the way she had come.

"Want me to bring you a tray?" Yerk called after her. "Corporal? *Corporal?*"

CHAPTER 25

The ride down the ice tunnel proved uneventful. Bloch kept the accelerator floored, but even downhill the golf cart seemed to drag its wheels, almost as if it knew something unpleasant lay ahead. But that was crazy.

Bloch sucked in a deep breath and felt the bite of cold air in his nostrils. *Crazier than aliens taking over a military base?* he wondered. *Crazier than the general and me sharing a psychotic breakdown?*

He took a couple more deep breaths and tried to slow the pounding of his heart. Why did this feel like the start of a panic attack?

You don't know anything yet. It's probably nothing. Just nerves. Just your imagination running away with you. Don't worry about it.

At last they reached the end of the tunnel. He circled the mini bulldozer and pulled to a stop before the tarp on the wall. General Wu hopped out before he switched off the golf cart's electric motor and set the hand brake.

Without any hesitation or fanfare, the general strode over to the tarp, grabbed a double handful of material, and yanked.

Both pitons holding it in place popped out and clattered to the floor. The canvas fell in what felt like a slow-motion cascade.

Bloch stared at the wall. It glistened, as smooth and slick and wet-looking as only melted ice could be. A dark cavity perhaps three feet tall and two feet wide extended into the wall. If anything had been inside, it certainly wasn't there now.

"Shit!" The general kicked the tarp. "Shit, shit, shit!"

Bloch found he had been holding his breath. He let it out with a shudder. The other shoe had fallen. At least now they knew—aliens really *were* loose on the base.

Or—was this part of their delusion?

Or—could it be another prank of some kind? Like the theft of their laptops?

He found himself nodding. Yes, that had to be it. Occam's razor.

If there had been a creature trapped in the ice, it couldn't still be alive. Not after millions of years. Never mind what the original report had said. It was physically impossible. Nothing could live that long.

He licked his lips. "Sir—"

"What?" Wu stopped cursing and kicking at the canvas. "Any thoughts, Colonel? Suggestions? Solutions?"

"Maybe—uh—maybe the soldiers took it out of the ice because they wanted selfies with it." He stared at the steering wheel in front of him, tightening his fingers around it until the knuckles turned white. He couldn't meet the general's hard gaze. "You know how they are. Maybe they just wanted, you know, a photo op."

"Don't play the fool, Ben. I expect better from you."

"Yes, sir." He sagged forward, hugging the steering wheel. Why did it feel like he'd just been kicked in the gut? Was it the missing alien or the general's anger and disappointment with him?

Wu walked stiffly back to the golf cart and dropped into the passenger seat. The golf cart rocked.

Bloch turned his head. The general's face had turned ashen. He was staring straight ahead, not speaking. Was he working on a plan?

"Sir? What next?" Bloch asked.

"I'd say we're fucked, but I can't allow myself to believe in a no-win scenario." He nodded. "We need options. Anything short of nuking the base—and maybe even that as a last resort." He gestured vaguely up the tunnel. "Drive. I need time to think."

"What about the tarp? Do you want me to put it back?"

The general snorted. "I don't think it matters now."

CHAPTER 26

It was like something from one of the nightmares she'd been having. An uncontrollable panic gripped her, an unthinking impulse to run and run and *run*. Usually in her dreams she found herself fleeing through endless corridors with unseen monsters snapping at her heels. No matter how fast she went, she couldn't pull away from them.

Now, as she turned right and fled toward the infirmary and the tunnel, she found herself not really thinking, just moving on autopilot. That one primal urge—*run, run, run!*—filled every fiber of her being.

If she glanced over her shoulder, she knew they'd be behind her. That pack of monsters, just like in her dreams—

She passed the infirmary door, turned left, and suddenly barrelled into someone. He staggered back with an "oof" and grabbed her shoulders with large, powerful hands. She looked up, saw kind brown eyes in a familiar face —

"Whoa, Corporal!" the man said.

She blinked, and abruptly she was conscious of being held at arm's length by Clay Washington. When she relaxed and tried to step back, he released her. She shivered, glanced over her shoulder. There was no one behind her. What had happened?

"Gonna hurt someone that way," he said. "You okay, Corporal?"

"Y-yes. Sorry. Thanks."

There were three of them, she realized. Clay and Terry, inseparable as always, and that new guy, Jase. They clustered around her, looking concerned, asking questions. She took a shuddering breath, glanced toward the mess hall again, shivered. Nobody there. No one had followed her out.

"Sorry," she said. She forced a laugh, but it sounded way too fake. What had made her run out the door that way? Had it been a panic attack? Of course, there weren't any monsters on an army base. Renner had just gotten inside her head, that was all. He had a way of doing that to everyone. The jerk.

She said, "I don't know what got into me. Suddenly I had to get out of the mess hall before…"

"Before what?" Jase asked.

She almost said, *Before they ate me.* But that sounded crazy. Like Renner and Seetoo would eat someone. She could have laughed at the thought. But right now, it didn't seem so crazy.

She ran fingers through her short-cropped hair and shook her head. How stupid did she look, running down the hallway like that? Better make a joke of it.

"It's just me. I got the creeps suddenly. You know."

It sounded lame as she said it. But they were all nodding, even Jase.

"I hear you," Washington said.

"Maybe it's low blood sugar," Terry said.

Jase said, "We were heading to the mess hall—"

"Don't go in there!" she blurted out then stopped herself. How crazy did *that* sound?

"What? Why?" Clay asked.

"Maybe you need to eat," Terry said. "Low blood sugar can do funny things to your brain chemistry."

I'm so hungry, she thought automatically. But she wasn't. Not really, not anymore.

She bit her lip, glanced over her shoulder toward the mess hall. Still no one in sight.

"That isn't it. This sounds insane, but…the people in there. There's something off about them. They're *not right.* Don't go in. Something bad will happen if you do. I don't know what, but I can feel it."

"Something bad?" Terry snorted. "It's lunch time! Did Dobbs put you up to this? Is it another one of his little jokes?"

"Do what you want. I'm not your mother." She gave a dismissive gesture. "It's your funeral."

Shouldering between them, she headed toward the women's barracks at a more controlled speed. After a half dozen steps, she began to jog. Then she began to run.

CHAPTER 27

"Corporal?" Nate called after Menendez one last time. But she was gone. He stared after her. What was her problem?

"Never mind her, Yerk," Kavanaugh said. He draped an arm around Nate's shoulders. "She'll join us soon enough. Come into the back. Everything's waiting for you."

"Yeah. Thanks."

So hungry— whispered a little voice in the back of his head.

Nate allowed himself to be steered toward the kitchen, but he kept glancing over his shoulder after the corporal. No sign of her returning—definitely weird. Who missed a meal? Then his stomach rumbled, reminding him of how hungry he was, and he grinned. *Chicken gumbo!*

All the others closed in behind him. At least he'd be first in line this time. No way did he want to miss the last of the biscuits.

But as he rounded the counter, he found the stove sitting there empty. Not a pot on a burner. Even the sink—normally piled full of pans and dishes—sat there clean and empty. He sniffed. Not a whiff of gumbo.

"Where's the grub?" He looked at Kavanaugh.

"Storeroom," said Seetoo.

"Storeroom," echoed Chuck Renner.

They both grabbed his arms and dragged him toward the storeroom.

"Guys, this isn't funny," he said.

He dug in his heels, but they were stronger than him, and they propelled him forward.

They dragged him past the walk-in freezer. The door to the storeroom stood ajar, and as they neared, he could see someone lying down inside. He could see only boots and part of a leg, but who would be lying down in there? Cookie?

"Guys?" he said again.

Then something warm and moist covered his mouth, and he

couldn't say another word. He began to struggle, but he couldn't break free. Why were they doing this? The colonel wouldn't be happy. He hated horsing around.

Kavanaugh shoved the storeroom door open the rest of the way. Seetoo and Renner rushed him inside, slamming him face-down on the floor. Breath whooshed from his lungs through his nose. He raised his head to call for help, but that warm, moist grip across his mouth never relaxed for even a second.

So hungry—

Twisting his head a little, he glimpsed half a dozen soldiers lying on the floor around him. But he couldn't make out who they were. Their faces were gone. Replaced by bloody, pulsing lumps of—*something*.

He gagged, felt vomit rising in his throat.

Couldn't move.

Couldn't breathe.

He rolled his eyes up. Took in the weird, writhing, alien *things* now hunched over the soldiers. Fleshy ropes connected them to the men and women. And in places their bodies seemed to merge together, as if they were becoming single beings.

This isn't real. This isn't possible.

He pressed his eyes shut.

And then the pain started like wildfire along his spine. It spread to his legs, his arm, his face.

He opened his mouth to scream, and the warm wetness flowed inside.

So hungry—

CHAPTER 28

"What was *that* about?" Jason asked, staring after her. Menendez raced by the storerooms, his office, then Bloch and Wu's offices. She didn't stop. She punched through the door at the end of the hallway and disappeared into the next building.

"No idea," Clay said. He scratched his head. "Normally she's the grown-up here. The whole base is acting screwy, if you ask me."

"I'm so hungry," Terry said, turning toward the mess hall, "I've got to eat. You know I suffer from low blood sugar."

"You heard what the corporal said." Jason trailed after him. "Maybe we should skip lunch. With all the weirdness, it might be safer."

So hungry. Terry's words echoed in his mind. He felt a faint pang of hunger in his own stomach. *So hungry—*

"Yeah," said Clay. "I got a bad feeling, too."

Jason stopped next to the infirmary door, and Clay paused beside him.

"I really need something. I'll just grab a snack and bring it with me." Terry started toward the mess hall. Over his shoulder, he added, "I need to eat, even if it's just a few crackers."

The moment he stepped into the doorway to the mess hall, a pair of what looked like flesh-colored bullwhips lashed out. One wrapped itself around his neck twice. The other pinned his arms to his sides. Both yanked him into the mess hall and out of sight.

In a heartbeat, he was gone. It had happened in utter silence.

Jason gaped. *What the hell?*

A loud, wet *crunch* followed, then a few *snap-snap* sounds, like breaking bones. Then a soft *thump*, like a body falling.

"Mother of God!" Clay whispered, grabbed his arm. "Terry—"

"Did you see—" Jase began.

He looked at Clay, who stared back at him with wide eyes.

The aliens were loose on the base. There could be no doubt now.

Without another word, Jase turned and sprinted after Corporal Menendez. Behind him, he heard Clay pounding at his heels.

CHAPTER 29

By the time Bloch drove the golf cart into the base, General Wu was sitting stiffly upright, a grimly determined look on his face. He had an idea, clearly. But what?

"Sir?" Bloch shifted in his seat. "Do you have a plan?"

"We have an advantage, Ben," the general said softly, like he'd just realized something important. He hopped out and started for the door into the base, shrugging off his jacket as he walked. "Think it through. Secrecy is the single greatest weapon of this species. They work most effectively when we're kept in the dark. They prey on isolated individuals, picking them off one at a time. They don't want to face organized resistance. They want to keep us ignorant and vulnerable."

"Granted. But how does that give us an advantage?"

"Basic strategy, Colonel. What do we have that they don't?"

Weapons? Superior fire-power? Bloch played through all the tactical advantages he could think of. It had been a long time since he'd studied such things.

Then it hit him—*information.*

He met the general's gaze. "We know about *them*—but *they* don't know it yet."

"Exactly. Until their cover is blown, or a tipping point is reached and they outnumber us, they will do everything they can to blend in. To pass as human. They won't risk attracting attention."

"But the laptops and the radio equipment—that attracted our attention."

"We dismissed the laptops as a prank. And they made the radio equipment's damage look like the work of an animal. Admit it, you had doubts."

"You're right." Bloch nodded slowly. He saw it now. The big picture. It wasn't pretty, but they still had a chance. But then the general's throwaway line about a tipping point hit him. *Until they outnumber us.* How long would that take?

Wu went on, "And, thanks to you, we have the perfect trap at hand."

"Me?" Bloch stared at him. He hadn't suggested a thing!

"Have you forgotten that Dr. Cosgrove wants to check the dump? I gave permission for him to search outside for more metal fragments."

"Outside. Yes." Bloch frowned. It all clicked into place. "The cold. It's sixty below. You'll order the aliens out to check the dump, then lock the doors. Once they're outside, we sit back and wait for the weather to do the rest."

"Like it did nineteen million years ago, when they first crashed here." The general smiled, but it wasn't a pleasant smile. "The best plans are the simplest ones, Colonel. Tomorrow morning, they'll be frozen stiff. *Then* we deal with them from a position of strength." He made a fist with his right hand and hammered it into his left palm. "All seven with one blow. We stack them up like cordwood, douse them with diesel fuel, and torch the lot. After they're gone, we chalk it down to lesson learned. We deal swiftly and decisively with any other aliens we find."

"You plan to continue digging? After everything that's happened?"

"I didn't come here to leave empty-handed."

That's why he's in command, Bloch thought. He'd always admired the general, but this pushed things to a whole new level. Wu saw the whole picture. How important alien technology could be to the United States. To mankind.

"Where do we start?".

"My office." Wu shoved through the door into the next building. "I have an announcement to make over the P.A. system."

CHAPTER 30

As they slammed through the door into the barracks section of the base, Jason caught Clay's arm and pulled him to a stop.

"What the hell happened to Terry?" Clay demanded.

"I don't know, and I don't want to find out," Jason said. He opened the door a crack and peeked into the corridor toward the mess hall. Deserted.

"See anything?" Clay pressed his face up against the crack, too.

"Nothing out of the ordinary." Jason eased the door closed as quietly as he could. Then he pointed to a round silver lock set into the door. It had a keyhole. "We need to find the key and lock whatever that was on the other side. I don't want it following us."

"I bet Bloch has the key."

"Yeah." Jason looked out again. Still nothing. "Maybe we can barricade the door in the meantime—"

He heard a sound behind them and whirled to see Colonel Bloch and General Wu coming through the door from the ice tunnel. Thank God!

"I'll tell them what happened," Clay said in a low voice. "Keep watch and shout if you see anyone. Or anything."

"Right."

Jason peeked out. Still no movement from the mess hall. This time he kept the door open an inch. He kept glancing over his shoulder every few seconds. Clay was talking and gesturing frantically, pointing toward Jason.

Then movement down the hallway caught his eye, and he tensed. Someone—the man's name was on the tip of his tongue, maybe Renner?—had just stepped out of the mess hall. He had what looked like a splash of blood across his left arm. Turning, he strolled at a leisurely pace toward Jason's door. Several others whose names Jason didn't know followed him out. They turned the other way and headed for the far end of the hall and the dormitories.

Jason closed the door and set his foot and shoulder against it.

"Someone's coming!" he called. "And a few more are going the other way."

A moment later, he felt pressure against the door, as though someone were leaning hard to push it open. He set his shoulder and leaned into the pressure. No way was he letting anyone through if he could help it.

"Come on, open up!" a man's voice called from the other side, sounding annoyed. "What're y'all doin' over there?"

"We're having some trouble with this door," Jason called. "Hinge broke. Give us five minutes to fix it!"

"Come on, I gotta take a leak!"

"Very funny," Jason called. "Latrine's the other way."

No reply. Had he given up? Gone back to the mess hall?

Suddenly Clay was standing next to him holding a brass key. He fitted it smoothly into the lock and gave it a sharp twist. Jason heard a deadbolt shoot home.

Renner must have heard it, too. A sudden loud *whump!* came, and the door shuddered, its surface vibrating. Jason leaped back. *Whump! Whump!* It sounded like an elephant pounding against the other side, not a man using fists.

Jason backed away, never taking his eyes from the door.

Whump! Whump!

"Bloch is going through the barracks to lock the door to the mess hall," Clay said. "Did you see how many headed around?"

"At least three. There's only one here—uh, I think his name is Renner?"

"Chuck Renner," Clay said. He leaned forward and called, "Hey, Chuck?"

"Yeah?" came the man's voice. The banging stopped

"There's a problem with the hinge, like Jase said. You aren't helping. Give us a few more minutes."

"That Clay Washington?"

"Yeah."

"Five minutes?"

"Yeah."

"...'Kay."

Jason swallowed and looked at Clay, who jerked his head toward the other end of the hall. Side by side, they hurried to where Wu stood by the door to the dorm building. Wu gazed toward the far end.

As they watched, Bloch locked the far door, sealing off the mess hall and the infirmary.

"Good man," Wu muttered, clearly speaking to himself. Then he seemed to notice them.

"What's going on?" Jason asked.

Wu looked down at the keyring he held, fiddled a small silver key off of it, and passed it over to Jason.

"What's this?" He took it.

"Bottom drawer of my desk. There's a cell phone, your laptop, and a Colt.45. Get them all. We're leaving."

Whump! Whump!

Jason jumped. The banging on the door had started again. He stared down the corridor. How long could the door last?

"It's Renner," Clay told the general.

Jason turned and sprinted to Wu's office, then with shaking hands managed to get the key into the desk's lock. He found a broken cell phone, pulled it out and put it into his pocket, then grabbed the laptop. Under it sat the Colt and several lumps of what looked like the ultra-light metal. He grabbed those, too, and stuffed them into his other pocket. Then, with the Colt in one hand and the laptop in his right, he ran back out to join Clay and the general.

Bloch emerged from the men's lavatory and shook his head. He mouthed the word, "Empty." Then he went into the men's dorm.

Wu glanced at Jason, then reached over and pried the pistol from his hand.

"I'll take that, if you don't mind."

A moment later, Bloch dashed frantically from the dorm room, with something clinging to his back like a jockey on a horse. Only the jockey was a sickly yellow-green color and had at least four hands wrapped across Bloch's face and chest, and it trailed what looked like the tentacles of a squid.

"Shit!" The general raised the pistol and fired four times. The first two hit the yellow squid-creature in what might have been its face, another hit its shoulder. The fourth hit Bloch square in the chest. He went down, and the creature hunched over him, its body pulsing like a human heartbeat.

"Back!" the general said. He grabbed the door and started to swing it closed.

At that moment, Corporal Menendez stepped out of the women's dorm. She looked at the Bloch and the creature, started to back up, then turned to run—and found Wu pointing his Colt at her forehead. She drew up short.

"Sir! It's me!" Eyes wide, she raised her hands.

"Whoa! Whoa!" Clay said, stepping past the general. "She's one of us! She warned us about the mess hall—"

General Wu hesitated a split second, then stepped back and motioned with the barrel of the pistol for Menendez to join them inside. She dashed past him, followed by Clay. Wu slammed the door shut.

He already had the key in the lock, Jason noticed, and he turned it to drive the deadbolt home. Now they were locked in. Trapped. But he'd locked aliens on the other side of both doors. At least for now.

Whump! Whump! Whump!

Jason almost jumped out of his skin when the pounding began again at the far end of the hallway. Renner hadn't waited. Or had five minutes already passed?

CHAPTER 31

"Was anyone else in the women's dorm with you?" Wu was demanding. Jason managed to focus on him.

"Just me," Menendez said. Her eyes stayed fixed on his pistol, even though he wasn't pointing it at her now.

"New plan," Wu said, turning and striding briskly the other way. "We take the chopper out. Follow me."

He started back up the hallway toward the door where Renner's pounding continued with no sign of slowing. Jason fell in behind Clay and the general. When he glanced back, he saw Menendez trailing, a dazed expression on her face. *She looks like I feel,* he thought.

They passed the first storeroom, then the radio room, then the second storeroom.

Jason couldn't escape the image of Bloch running at them with that alien thing on his back. It played over and over in his mind, an endless, horrible loop. At least the doors to the other sections of the base didn't have windows. Somehow, he didn't want to see what was happening on the other side.

"Can you fly it?" he heard Clay asking the general.

Wu glanced at him. "In theory. I've seen it done a thousand times, and I have the basic concepts down. I don't see a better option."

"Forget that," said Clay. "No way am I going up with an untrained pilot. I'll do it."

"You fly?" Jason asked him.

He glanced back. "Hell, yeah! My dad was a pilot for Delta. I had my commercial license at 19. In college, I flew a weather copter for KSOT St. Louis for two years." He barked a laugh. "All news, all the time. They should have *this* for a scoop!"

The general gave a curt nod. "Fine. You're the pilot. Let's go."

Jase slowed enough to let them get ten feet head, then paused and motioned for Menendez to stop, too.

"The copter isn't going to work," he said in a low voice.

"How do you know?"

"The aliens have been one step ahead of us the whole time. They sabotaged the radio room and stole Bloch's and Wu's laptops. I bet you anything they got to the helicopter, too. That's where I would have started. Nothing to permanently damage it, just something to keep it grounded unless one of them is in the cockpit. Maybe the equivalent of removing the spark plugs. If they even have spark plugs these days."

"Makes sense." She glanced toward the general. He and Clay were still talking, Jason saw, and hadn't yet realized they'd stopped.

He asked, "Can you think of another way off the base?"

She frowned. "Maybe. But you aren't going to like it."

"Try me."

"We have a mini bulldozer in the tunnel. It's not fast, but it's been modified to run in sub-zero temperatures. We could load it with a couple of barrels of fuel from the outside depot. That should be enough to get us several hundred miles, if we're lucky."

"Why do I hear a 'but' coming?"

"There's only one 'dozer. And it seats one person. We're both pretty small, so I could probably sit on your lap to drive. But Clay and the general? No way will they fit, too."

"Then the chopper is the only viable way for all of us to get out." He didn't make it a question.

"You better hope you're wrong about the sabotage."

He sucked in a deep breath and picked up his pace. "Come on. We don't want to be left behind."

He had almost caught up with the general and Clay when they entered the little airlock-room that opened onto the helicopter pad at the center of the base. Then the general turned and without warning slammed the door in Jason's face. Jason heard the telltale click of the deadbolt. What the hell?

He grabbed the door handle, twisted it, shoved—but the door wouldn't budge. Locked from the other side.

Jase pounded on it. "Open up, you bastard!" he yelled. "Wu! Damn you! Open the goddamn door!"

"Can't take any chances," he heard Wu call through the door. "You and Menendez were out of my sight, so I can't be sure about you. It's nothing personal. The survival of humanity depends on me reaching help. I wish you both good luck."

Jason stepped back and kicked the door. "Bastard!"

"Fuck him," Menendez said. Turning, she jogged to the double doors leading to the ice tunnel and pushed one open. "I'll get the 'dozer. Start putting on cold gear—as many layers as you can manage. You're about Kavanaugh's size. Start with his suit. It's gonna to be a bitch of a ride."

Jason nodded. He shot a last glare in the general's direction, then stomped after her.

Thermal jackets, gloves, ski masks, and goggles were in cubbies along the wall. He found the one labeled PFC Kavanaugh and grabbed a black jacket from the hook.

CHAPTER 32

As Wu stepped away from the door, he felt a twinge of regret. He liked Menendez and had come to respect Dr. Cosgrove. But he couldn't take any chances, especially with the corporal. The stakes were too high at this point. She had been alone in the women's barracks. No telling whether the aliens had gotten to her.

He shrugged. Nothing to be done about it now—he was committed. Taking a deep breath, he pushed them from his mind. Time to focus on the copter and escape.

He grabbed his coat from its peg and started to shrug it on. But then he heard a strange gurgling behind him. A cold, pricking sensation went down his back. He stiffened, fingers dropping to the pistol tucked into his belt.

Then he whirled, drawing the Colt in a fluid motion. Good thing he'd saved two bullets when he shot the creature on Bloch's back. He jerked it up and aimed—but half a second too slow. He realized his mistake when he saw Clay Washington.

Clay's body rippled and flowed like some weird half-liquified putty. His arms stretched toward Wu, lengthening, transforming into something like fleshy ropes or tentacles, only dark and smooth. One whipped out and caught his hand, pinning it and the pistol against the wall. The other punched against his chest and knocked him hard against the door. He heard more than felt ribs break.

"When did they get you?" he gasped. It sounded stupid the moment he said it. So much for famous last words.

"I went to the latrine in the middle of the night," the mouth said, its words coming out as a wet mumble. That mouth was the last facial feature remaining. Clay's eyes, nose, and ears had already melted flat against what should have been a skull but wasn't. "It was over fast, General. Don't resist. It won't hurt as much."

Wu struggled to turn the Colt in his hand. If he could shift it enough to target the thing's head—

Before he could shoot, Clay's whole body split apart like an overripe melon from skull to crotch. From inside the chest cavity, dozens of thin, white tendrils lashed up and out. They whipped toward Wu's face. Each tendril had a cluster of tiny suckers at its tip, and each sucker had a wickedly barbed hook at its center. As the hooks pierced his cheeks and eyes, Wu tried to scream. But more tendrils filled his mouth and throat, and he gagged on a sudden gush of warm blood.

His hand spasmed. Distantly, he heard two shots echo through the room.

Pop. Pop.

Like firecrackers at Chinese New Year.

Then darkness had him.

CHAPTER 33

The mini bulldozer ground its way up the ramp slightly faster than a man could walk. Corporal Menendez hunched over the steering wheel, her foot pressing the accelerator to the floor, even though she knew she couldn't coax more speed from its rumbling treads. The little machine had been built for power, not racing. It only had two gears—forward and reverse.

Finally, after what seemed an eternity, she rounded the last switchback, and the base came into view. A bulky, over-bundled figure stood at the top of the ice ramp waiting for her. Jase, in Kavanaugh's gear. She drove the 'dozer to the top, swerved around Jase, and stopped in front of the large outside door.

Putting the 'dozer in park, she called, "Open the door while I get dressed!" to Jase, then dashed over to her cubby. She had a black thermal coat and pants, which she donned over her uniform. Then she pulled on a black ski mask, goggles, and gloves. She hesitated a second, then grabbed four packs of thermal blankets—the thin silver ones—from the emergency supply case. They were meant for anyone suffering from hypothermia, but they might prove useful on the trip. Then she grabbed a handful of flares and two bottles of water. If they needed more to drink than that, they weren't going to make it anyway.

She glanced at Jase. He had finally figured out the door controls and was holding down the large red button that operated the machinery. A low-pitched *beep-beep-beep* warned that the outside door was being opened, and as it slid to the left, a searing blast of cold rushed in. She felt it even through her insulated clothing.

Outside, the wind was rising, and it made a low hissing sound as it swept across the ice. The sun, a small white ball, hung low in the sky. It provided no real heat here.

She adjusted her goggles to best protect her eyes, then tramped back to the 'dozer. There, she took a minute to wedge the blankets and flares behind the driver's seat before tucking one of the water bottles inside her coat so it wouldn't freeze. Then she rolled up the 'dozer's side windows using the hand cranks and switched on its tiny heater. Every little bit of heat counted out here.

Jason joined her. "What next?"

She handed him a bottle of water. "Put this under your coat, as close to your skin as you can get it. If it freezes, you won't be able to drink it."

"Good idea."

She watched as he unzipped his jacket and stuck it inside as fast as he could. From just that three-second exposure to the Antarctic cold, though, he was already shivering.

"The fuel depot is to the left." She pointed out the door. "Follow me out and we'll load up. I think we can get two barrels in the shovel and maybe another two behind the cab."

"Will it freeze?"

"I hope not."

Hopping into the driver's seat, she slammed the door and drove out.

Wind swirled bits of snow and ice across the ground ahead of her. When she first got to the base, she had liked to watch its ever-changing patterns through the mess hall windows. But that had been before the nightmares started. Now the ice and snow and cold had all lost any charms it once had.

The fuel depot was a low steel shed perhaps twenty feet from the main building. She drove as close to it as she could, then lowered the shovel. Just a matter of wrangling the fuel barrels into place.

Hopping down, she crossed to the shed's door and pulled it open by hand. She flipped the light switch, and fluorescent lights hanging from the ceiling came to life, revealing hundreds of barrels of diesel fuel. Each was about two feet tall and weighed nearly a hundred pounds.

She pointed to the barrels on the left side of the building. "Those are full."

With Jase's help, she tipped the closest onto its side and rolled it toward the 'dozer. Jase wasn't nearly as strong as any of the enlisted men—he probably didn't work like they did—but they managed to get it into the shovel. Repeating the process, they got a second one seated next to the first.

As they paused to catch their breath, she saw him glance toward the base. Wondering about Wu?

"Come on, let's get one more," she said. The faster they finished, the sooner they could be out of here.

He nodded and trudged along beside her as she went back to the shed.

They had no luck trying to get the next barrel to stay on the back of the 'dozer. Just as the machine hadn't been built for speed, it hadn't been built for cargo, either. The barrel kept sliding off no matter how they tried to brace it in place.

"This isn't going to work," she finally told Jase after their fourth try.

"Do you think we have enough fuel to make it?" he asked.

"It's gotta be enough."

He glanced toward the base again.

"Did you hear the helicopter while I was in the tunnel?" she asked.

"No."

"Then you were right. It must have been sabotaged. It shakes the whole building when it lands or takes off. No way would you have missed it."

"So General Wu didn't get to ditch us." He sagged a little.

"He would have." She smiled grimly behind her ski mask. "Small comfort, though. Like I said, fuck him. And fuck Clay, too, for going along with it. Serves 'em both right. Bastards."

"Yeah."

"Come on, get inside." She opened the 'dozer's door and motioned him into the cab. "Time to hit the road."

He climbed up and into the driver's seat. As he settled himself, she pushed the control to lower the seat. It dropped an inch. He reached down between his legs, found the bar to move the seat back, and shoved with his legs until it locked into place. It only gave them a few more inches, but it would have to do.

Jase stuck out his hand. Grabbing his wrist, she hauled herself up and perched on his lap. Her feet could just reach the gas pedal, and the steering wheel pressed into her stomach a bit, but she'd been right—she could drive it this way.

She slammed the door shut, reached instinctively for the seatbelt, then dropped it. No way would it reach around both of them.

"What's the plan?" Jase asked.

"There's a Swedish science base about two hundred miles from here. I've seen it on the station's maps. It has something to do with monitoring climate change, I think. Hopefully it's still there and still manned. If not…we'll go to Plan B."

"Plan B?"

"Improvise."

He laughed. "Plan B. I like it."

She pulled the lever on the right, raising the mini bulldozer's shovel until it was eight feet off the ground. Then, mindful of the fuel barrels cradled overhead, she backed clear of the shed, put the 'dozer in drive, turned to the right—and floored it.

The treads growled with power. The little heater whirred. At a stately eight miles per hour, they rumbled toward the sun.

Two hundred miles. Twenty-five hours of driving.

She swallowed hard. They could do it.

They had to.

EPILOG

The plane from Amundsen-Scott Station touched down lightly on the Christchurch runway. Its landing wheels bumped twice more before the sheer weight of the vehicle pressed it safely to the ground. Engines roared into reverse. Passengers pressed forward hard against their seatbelts as they decelerated.

The plane taxied for a few minutes before coming to a stop. When its engines shut down, silence settled over the cabin. Pilot and copilot emerged from the cockpit and, without a word, began undogging the hatch on the left side of the cabin.

Soldiers began to unbuckle and stand, removing duffle bags from overhead racks and shouldering them.

Dull metallic clangs sounded outside. The copilot swung the hatch open. A set of steel mesh steps had already been wheeled over to the airplane. Workers in bright orange coveralls, with noise-dampening headphones over their ears, gave exaggerated waves of welcome. The copilot waved back. Then he picked up his small suitcase by the handle and exited.

The pilot followed with his own suitcase. Then, one by one, the soldiers filed out and down the steps in a silent line.

The last to leave the plane paused for a second at the top of the steps, gazing around the Christchurch airport. The sun rode high overhead; he squinted as eyes, accustomed to the dimmer illumination of the cabin, adjusted to sudden brightness. A cold, steady breeze blew in from the west. Smells of diesel exhaust and sun-warmed asphalt overrode any scents from the surrounding countryside, but in the distance the green of growing things could be seen, along with a scattering of buildings and the movement of a handful of cars and trucks on a nearby road.

Slowly, the thing that had been General Wu smiled.

The story will continue with Book 2

Mars Is Hell

by John W. Campbell, Jr.
and John Gregory Betancourt